# upstream
## melissa lion

WENDY
LAMB
BOOKS

Published by Wendy Lamb Books
an imprint of Random House Children's Books
a division of Random House, Inc.
New York

This is a work of fiction. Names, characters, places, and incidents either are the product of the author's imagination or are used fictitiously. Any resemblance to actual persons, living or dead, events, or locales is entirely coincidental.

www.randomhouse.com/teens

Educators and librarians, for a variety of teaching tools, visit us at
www.randomhouse.com/teachers

The Library of Congress has cataloged the hardcover edition of this work as follows:
Lion, Melissa.
Upstream / Melissa Lion.
p. cm.
Summary: After her boyfriend is killed in a hunting accident,
Alaska high-school-senior Marty, with help from her mother and two
younger sisters, tries to get over her grief and begin a new life.
ISBN-13: 978-0-385-74643-4 (trade) — ISBN-13: 978-0-385-90877-1 (library binding)
ISBN-10: 0-385-74643-1 (trade) — ISBN-10: 0-385-90877-6 (library binding)
[1. Grief—Fiction. 2. Family Life—Alaska—Fiction. 3. Death—Fiction. 4. Alaska—
Fiction. 5. High schools—Fiction. 6. Schools—Fiction.] I. Title. PZ7.L6633Up 2005
[Fic]—dc22
2004015145
ISBN-13: 978-0-375-83954-2 (trade pbk.)
ISBN-10: 0-375-83954-2 (trade pbk.)

Book design by Angela Carlino

Printed in the United States of America

10 9 8 7 6 5 4 3 2 1

First Trade Paperback Edition

# upstream

Also by Melissa Lion

*swollen*

For my mom, Linda Helbock

A true, true Alaska girl

Thank you to my agent, Loretta Barrett.
And to Wendy Lamb and Alison Meyer, both of
whom believe in beauty.

# Fall

I've snuck into his house through the window he snuck
out of so many nights. It is nearly midnight, but it's the last
day of summer, and so the night sky is a burning purple,
the final moments of sunset. Not the deep black of the winter night. I know I should be home, in my own bed, waiting
for morning, for the first day back to school. But I want
to be with him, though I know he's not here. The house is
completely empty of him, his mom, his brother. All of them
are gone—furniture, posters, sounds of boys laughing. But
there are shreds of them left in this house. There is a smell
of wet leaves and dirt—the smell of him after he ran across
the field of fireweed to my window in the dark. As I kneel

on the floor, in the blue light I see streaks from sneakers and hiking boots and waders. And I stand and face the huge diamond-shaped window that looks out at the bay and to Iliamna, a pulsing blue peak two hundred miles away.

He was there, close to me, his arms around me, whispering like he had so many times. "Iliamna, that's you. Redoubt is Dottie, and Spurr is Gwen. The three sisters," he said, his arm over my shoulder, pointing at the range that looked so close because of its size. Iliamna was closest and looked the largest but was the shortest of the three. And Spurr was just a smudge in the sky, but it was the tallest peak on the range.

I turn from the window and drag my finger in the dust. Spiderwebs pull and pop as I break their delicate holds.

I open my sleeping bag and take off my shoes. I climb in with my jeans on. As I lay my head on my bunched-up sweatshirt, I catch a glimpse of a light in the cottonwood near my house. I drag the sleeping bag to the window and look closer, squinting. From the ground I can see our fort. I didn't know it could be seen. When we were kids, Dottie and I had checked it from the car and from a cottonwood across the field and it was never visible. But here on the floor of his house, I can see right to it. And inside there is a candle burning.

Dottie started disappearing during the day while Mom was at work and Gwen had a playdate and I was supposed to be cleaning or cooking or reading when all I really wanted to do was lie in bed and stare at the ceiling. She'd been fixing it. She'd been turning it back into a fort, instead of some planks of wood weathered and rotting in a tree.

I knew she had fixed it well. She had built our shed and the shelves in the garage. She often said she would build her own log cabin one day. And this was her first attempt.

The candle burns bright in the little fort. It flickers and throws shadows, and then it is still again. She is up there with Sean. The boy she loves, but always says she doesn't. She is with him in the night, though she never agrees to bring him to the movie theater or goes with him to dances. And everyone at school knows they're a couple, though she never sits with him and never holds his hand. I watch that candle and as I grow sleepy, my eyes nearly shut, I see what I know will happen. The candle almost flickers out and then burns as bright as the sun, the whole tree lit, and for just one moment that fort burns, and then the fire fades back to a candle flame, and then two fingers reach out to snuff that final bit of light.

I know it will happen because it used to be that way for me and Steven, when we were alone in the night. The two of us under his tent in the back of his truck. Or alone in the movie theater if I had worked the closing shift. I know that burning, and now that he's gone, I know I'll never have it again.

I wake early with the rising sun. I roll my sleeping bag, put my shoes on and walk down the road to my house. It's silent inside, Mom gone to work, my sisters still asleep. I check on Gwen, who's drooled a large spot on her pillow in the night, and see Dottie tucked in, peaceful. Without her makeup she looks like the little girl she used to be. She looks like Gwen. I shower and make tea and eggs for them and slowly they wander in.

"Morning, girlies."

"Morning, Marty," says Gwen, and kisses me with sticky lips.

"Sister," says Dottie.

"Dorothy Ann," I say, and kiss the top of her head. She grunts and tries to dodge me, but I put my arms around her just to drive her crazy. She smells like a campfire.

"I hope everyone is ready for a new school year. Gwen, more boys for you to chase with scissors, and Dottie, with so many days to ditch ahead of you, how do you stand it?"

Dottie raises her mug of tea to her lips and with the other hand gives me the finger behind Gwen's back.

Gwen is scooping eggs into her mouth, and I sit with them and push my eggs around, because for the first time I am scared to go to school. I'm scared because Steven won't be there and everyone will know, they'll know what happened and why I'm sitting by myself.

My sisters finish and I wash the plates and yell at them to get ready faster. Gwen needs her jeans rolled—Mom bought them too big. I find Dottie back in bed and have to sit on her butt to get her out again.

"You suck." Her face is stuffed into the pillow.

"You too, though more often, like last night."

She rolls over, heaving me off the bed. "Martha, don't even try it. Mom would never believe you anyway."

"Just get up," I say, and slam her door, though I'm not mad, and I'm not going to tell Mom. I just want her to get up, because I'm not walking into school alone.

I drive the Jeep with the top pulled back and the heater on and I know I drive too fast. Flower bouquets and crosses line the road. Head-ons, black ice, cars driving off the road.

But we're late and I hate being the reason for it. We pull up to Gwen's school and she jumps out, her backpack loaded and drooping. She waves and turns.

"She looks like a beetle," Dottie says. And she does and I want to cry, seeing her go, though she doesn't turn. She loves school. She loves the kids there. She voluntarily took summer classes, painting and Spanish and drama, though none really interested her. She came home with stories about the kids and the teacher and herself.

"Bye, beetle butt," I call.

She runs back to the car and kisses me again, this time with minty lips, and she turns and runs to the door.

"Ready, sis?" says Dottie, and puts her hand on mine.

"No."

"It's okay. They've had all summer to get used to it."

"I hope so. Where's your makeup?" It's the first time I've noticed that she isn't wearing her normal war paint. Her lips are glossy and pale, and her deep blue eye shadow is gone.

"Natural look this year."

"How long did it take to put the natural look on?"

"A little less than the mob moll look I used to work."

"You look pretty."

"I think you'd look prettier with your foot on the pedal and your hand on the shift."

"Too sweet." I pull out and squeal the tires on the driveway. Let them think even worse things about us. The three sisters and our mom living alone. Dad coming home only once in a while without warning when his Coast Guard ship docks.

• • •

The front of school is crowded and I hope we can just slip in, but as we walk past clusters of kids, conversations slow and stop. Hands cover mouths as they gossip.

"It's my eye shadow," Dottie says, and takes my arm. She's right, I tell myself, but I walk with my head down into the main hall, where I stop and look around, quickly passing my eyes over all those familiar faces. I look up to the ceiling where my whale is.

Despite everything, all that I am now, it is still there. The plaque next to it describes the process—how it went from a carcass on the beach to this gleaming white skeleton hanging from the ceiling of a high school. The National Science Fair award is there too. And the photo, black-and-white and framed. It is a picture of all the kids who worked on the bones, cleaning, recording, piecing them together. There were fifty of us who always showed up, with about twenty more who passed in and out of the warehouse once we started putting the whale back together.

And in the center of the photo (I know I shouldn't pause and look so the others can look at me) there's Steven and me. He has his arms out and his palms spread. His mouth is open. He was yelling my name, trying to get the others to say *Martha* instead of *whales*. And there I am, looking away, looking at a girl who kneels below me. She was saying *cheese,* and I remember wondering if it really matters what you say when the photo is being taken. If you smile, you smile. And now, looking at that photo, I see her smile is much wider than those around her. I look close and I'm not smiling at all.

I'd found the whale on the beach, at the end of the spit. I was there for no particular reason; it was nearly winter, a

Sunday. Dottie was gone for the day, and Gwen was at the neighbors' while Mom shopped in Anchorage. This was before I met Steven, though it led him to me. I was walking and skipping rocks and the ocean was churning gray; a storm hung heavy across the water. I knew I had time to skip some rocks before the rain started. I held a smooth gray stone in my palm, already warm from my touch. I was kneeling, waiting for a small wave to stop lapping at the shore, and as I glanced back down the beach I saw the large bulk in the distance. It was foggy, so I wasn't sure. The wind began to howl, and I knew the rain was getting close. I had no top on the Jeep, but I went to that big gray lump on the beach. I smelled it before I could make out the shape. It was a sour smell, sharp, but not the smell of death like the riverbanks in August with the salmon skeletons covering the shores and hovering in the shallows. It smelled like the sea, like I imagined the bottom of the ocean would smell.

When I was close enough to see that it was a whale, I could tell that nature had already begun its slow cleaning. The birds had gotten the eyes, and flies blanketed the mouth. And I was sad for that whale. It had traveled very far. It had found the deepest, darkest depths, and small holes in the ice to breathe from. It had found mates, and mothers, but had somehow gotten lost in the open water, so lost it wound up in Cook Inlet and now, dead on the beach. It wasn't giant—no blue whale, no humpback. Just a small white whale. Young, maybe.

The drops started falling and I knew I had to leave before I too got washed away. I ran back up the beach and into the Jeep.

I drove home, and that storm reached me as I slammed the door and ran to the house. I stayed quiet during dinner, thinking about the whale, hoping no one else would find it. It was cold, and the spit rats, the college kids who camped there in the summer, were gone. The heavy storm brought darkness much earlier than normal, and so I was confident the next day when I went straight to the science teacher and told him about the whale.

We got donations from local businesses to fund the project, and people lent us tools and trucks and a warehouse. And one day, as we were bleaching the bones, Steven walked in. He'd been in a class of mine a year earlier, and I knew he was my neighbor. His mother brought us zucchini bread each Christmas. When I saw him at school, he always had a book in his hand. Sometimes I wouldn't see him for weeks.

"Can I help?" he asked me. He'd sought me out.

"You have to talk to Mr. King."

"It's your whale. I'm asking you." I noticed his eyes were the bright, opaque blue of glacier water.

"Everyone's welcome. We're still cleaning it; we haven't gotten to putting it back together yet. It's not great work, but it will look good on your college applications." This was why most of the kids were there.

He nodded and looked around. He bit his lip and maybe that was why I said, "Work next to me." And I was glad I did. He cleaned each inch as if it were a museum relic, and yet it was just a whale. "Martha's whale," he called it, though he was the only one.

Dottie grabs my hand and I am back in school. The first day. "Marty, we have to go. You're in AP History. You remember how to get to Mr. Martin's class?" Dottie looks worried, her perfectly arched brows pressing together. I haven't seen her look like that since the days just after Steven.

I am hunched over the photo again. There is more to look at. There's Steven's shirt—which one is it? Is it the one I gave him for his birthday, the one with a single blue stripe across the chest, or is it the shirt he called his tough-guy shirt, the one that made him look broader in the shoulders?

"Marty. History. Go." She nudges me, and I stumble.

I turn back to the picture, but I can't find him again. I've looked too close and now he's gone. I begin to straighten up and I hear my sister tell someone, "She's still spacing out. Sometimes she doesn't even hear me."

"I heard you," I say. "Class. I'm not retarded. Sean, so good of you to sleep with my sister in my childhood tree-house."

Sean blushes a deep red and he steps away from Dottie as Dottie rolls her eyes at him. She would never touch that hot skin to cool it, like Steven used to touch mine when I blushed. And normally I would blush talking about my sister's sex life like I just did, but there is no blush there, no heat in my cheeks.

"Martha, you need to get going. Please," she says, stepping right in front of me. She looks me in the eye, worried again, and I can't take another moment of her worrying. I can't know she has anything to worry about.

"Okay, I'm off like a prom dress."

"Now you're speaking my language." Dottie leans in quick before she can decide against this and kisses me on the cheek. The campfire smell is gone, replaced by tea roses.

I walk fast, grateful that the halls are clear. The final bell rings as I walk into class. Everyone is still talking, and Mr. Martin lets them talk until I take my seat. I sit in the aisle closest to the door, away from the window seat Steven sat in last year. "If I lean far enough while Martin has his back to us, I can see your mountain from my seat," he'd said.

From my seat, all I can see is woods, the dead conifers on the outside, gray and falling, and deep inside, the green of the forest. The conifers are dying this year. They'll be gone before long. A bark beetle is taking over, and people are worried, cutting them down. But this is just one type of tree that has grown here. There are more, different trees that will replace these.

A girl behind me whispers—I hear "camping" and "bears"—and I stiffen. But then I hear "Kodiak Island" and I know she is just telling a story. Maybe Dottie was right. They've had all summer to forget.

Mr. Martin goes over the general schedule for the class. He asks us about the books we read all summer, and he doesn't call on me, though he looks at me when other students are talking. He smiles and nods, and when class is over he passes my desk and squeezes my shoulder.

I won't cry as he leaves my row, as a girl knocks into me with her backpack. I won't cry, because I spent my summer crying. I cried and drove. I drove late, after midnight; the sun was still bright in the sky, so I drove even later. I cried in the shower. I cried and Gwen's sticky kisses didn't help and Dottie's tight, rare hugs didn't stop me. I cried and Mom took a week off from her job. She works on the roads in Alaska—one of the Northern Dames, an all-female road construction union. She was supervising a project on a patch of Sterling Highway damaged from last year's rains.

But she took a week off and sent Gwen to summer camp, and Dottie to Sean's. I cried her whole vacation, but she sat with me, wearing sweatpants in the middle of the day when normally she'd be in jeans. She'd sit with her legs tucked beneath her, twirling a single piece of her short black hair between her fingers, and watch me while I cried.

She'd hand me water, and a fresh tissue, and rarely say a word. She didn't offer advice, and she didn't tell me things would get better.

"Just get it out. I'll wait," she said. And she did. She brought me into town for errands and let me sit in the car. When she drove, I'd cry. She'd put her arm around me, even though she'd swerve into the other lane.

"Look out," I said once.

"Right now, do you really care if I swerve into this lane? Do you really care if a car is coming the other way?" she asked.

"I don't," I said, and she nodded, keeping her arm right where it was.

"I'll leave the crying to you, and you leave the driving to me."

And I put my head on her shoulder, the flannel of her shirt soft under my cheek. I hadn't rested on her in years, but it felt so good, with my hot tears running down my face.

And at the end of her vacation, the morning of her first day back, I made eggs. I let one single tear drip into the scramble and then stopped. I'd cried all my tears. I didn't feel better, but I was able to stop. I was able to see. I could walk outside and see the glaciers and the cottonwoods and the sandhill cranes, and for a moment I wouldn't be sad.

The classroom is clear. Mr. Martin erases dates and chapters from the board.

"Marty," he says as I pass, "I meant to ask you, and I just never have. How did you guys hoist that skeleton and secure it to the ceiling?"

He is wearing a tie and collared shirt. The tie is a Hawaiian print. I remember Steven told me that by Christmas Mr. Martin would be wearing full-on Hawaiian shirts. "It makes him feel better about the darkness," Steven said.

"Kids from the engineering department at the university came over. They told us what they needed and took measurements, then rigged it up. They got credit too, I think."

We'd lifted it just a few days before school let out. It was the same day the photo was taken. Steven stood behind me, his hands on my shoulders, while the ropes tightened in the pulleys and the whale left the ground.

"Look at what you did," he said as they lifted. "Amazing."

"We all did it. You did it too."

"No, we were all following you."

We were already in love by then. I knew that burning feeling Dottie learned last night. He really did believe that whale was all my doing.

Mr. Martin replaces the eraser. "Interesting. I like looking at it as I come to work. I'm glad you guys did it."

"Thank you," I say.

He nods again and sighs, looking out the window Steven had looked out of. I have to leave, though there is more I want to say to Mr. Martin. He was Steven's favorite teacher. And Mr. Martin cried at the funeral. He wore a black suit and a deep blue tie. He sat by himself in the fifth row and wept during the eulogy. He was in front of me in the line as we offered our condolences to his mom and brother. I watched him, trying to see what I should do. How I was supposed to act. He whispered into her ear, his hand on her elbow. And he hugged Steven's brother tight. I didn't know what to do when it was my turn. I hugged his brother fast. He was antsy, tired of being touched, and so he dropped his arms and let me let him go. I hugged his mom but she held on. "We're Alaska girls. You and me. We'll be okay." And she released me. Mr. Martin led me away, his arm around me, delivering me back to my mom and Dottie.

And now, as Mr. Martin stares at the trees and beyond, at the mountains, I worry that anything I have to say will make him weep again, and that will make me start, and like I said, I have cried enough. I have cried my share.


Dottie is waiting for me for lunch. We find Sean sitting alone, behind the school, away from the crowd. He has a napkin laid out for Dottie and one for me, and he takes out sandwiches for the three of us.

"Thanks, Sean," I say as he unwraps the wax paper for me. I often wondered where Dottie went for lunch. I thought she and Sean left campus to make out in his car, but now I know they had picnics, and it isn't a bad picnic spot. The grass is dry, and there is a view of Kachemak Bay.

"My mom made it for you guys. She said she saw you at the market and you looked too thin."

I look down at my pants; earlier in the week I borrowed a belt from Dottie to cinch them up. "I'm okay."

"Well, my mom said you're always welcome to eat. You can come over anytime." He looks down into his food and pulls at the cuff of his pants and Dottie puts a hand on his knee. It is the first time I've seen them touch when they know someone can see. And I see my sister look at him with a small smile, a smile like Steven would give if I caught his eye over a whale bone, or through a row of kids in class.

"I will," I say. "Can I bring my sister? I think you'd like her."

"I think Gwen's a little young for me," he says, and pinches Dottie's hand.

"She's the only honorable one I have left."

"Why do you think I'd want an honorable girl?" he asks, and a smile breaks over his face.

"What guy does?" asks Dottie with a shrug. She bites into her sandwich.

Sean tells me about the moose blind he and his dad camped in all week. "Not a single shot. A couple of cows passed beneath us, but they're not regulation. We sat up there for a full seven days."

"I bet you had to pee when you got down," says Dottie.

"Like you can't imagine."

I am grateful for this conversation, happy for a few moments when words can just wash over me. Sean is simply talking. He isn't worrying about whether he's saying things that might offend me, whether he's being unsympathetic. The bell rings and I'm not ready to leave. There is so much more normal conversation I want to have. There is so much I missed over the summer.

And so I drop Dottie and Sean off at their English class.

"Hey, Martha." A girl's voice comes from behind me, and a soft touch on my elbow.

I turn. My friend Jen smiles at me. "Hey," she says again. "Class?"

"Few minutes," I say. I've known her most of my life. Since at least kindergarten, when she'd play with me when Dottie was sick or away at camp. Her mom worked with my mom. At Steven's funeral she hugged me once and told me to call when I was ready. I feel bad now, seeing her after never calling.

"Sorry we haven't talked."

She waves her hand, erasing my apology. "I'm a rock star now." She laughs.

"They playing you on MTV?"

"That's the next step. For now, I'm entertaining the masses at Latitude 59. Friday nights. I'd like you to come."

She plays guitar and sings songs about love, though I've never seen her with a boy. She played last year at the talent show, her eyes closed, no need for a mike. And Steven had leaned over to me. "She'll be big one day. Listen to the voice."

I closed my eyes and at first just heard the sound of my childhood friend. A moment with both of us holding hairbrushes up to our mouths singing a ballad to a boy on television.

"It's like the color of burgundy velvet," he whispered in my ear.

And it was.

"Open mike?" I say.

"No, my own set. All to myself," Jen says.

I look away from her. It's been more than a year since I've seen her play. That's not how I should treat a friend.

The final bell rings. "I don't think the teachers will believe we got lost on the way to class," Jen says, and touches my arm again. "Come to the café. It's fun, and maybe I'll sign an autograph."

"And maybe I'll tell your adoring fans about the time you puked popcorn and chocolate milk through your nose after too much time in the tire swing."

"Perfect," she says with a wink, and opens the door to the ceramics studio. Last year, the ceramics students made missing bones for the whale.

"See you soon," I say at my own door, and smile. One friend, who's not obligated to me by blood.


Mom is home when we return from school. Gwen is talking about the frog her teacher promised to dissect as soon as the school year gets under way.

"Gwen, you dissect salmon all the time. What's so great about a frog?" says Dottie. I'm thinking the same thing.

"I've never cut open a frog. It's different than a salmon. It has feet."

Mom is in the kitchen breading pork chops. She usually naps for a bit after work because she has to be at the site by four in the morning, and Dottie and I fix dinner. But sometimes she surprises us.

"Hello, my pretties," she says as we pile into the kitchen.

"I'm going to cut open a frog," says Gwen.

"Save the legs for dinner," says Mom. "How was the first day back?" she asks, drying her hands on a towel. This is why she's home. She wants to make sure I'm okay. That no one has pestered me. When I was in the second grade—the same age Gwen is now—a girl stole my jacket. She told me it was lost, and then wore it the next day. The teacher said she thought it was the other girl's jacket to begin with. Mom showed up during recess, snuck into school and took the jacket out of the classroom while no one was looking. She left a note in the girl's cubby: *Thank you for my nice warm jacket, A Starving Child in Siberia.*

She gave the jacket to Dottie, who was a grade lower than I was, and on a different recess schedule. And she bought me a brand-new jacket with my name stitched on the breast.

"Good," I say. "I have Mr. Martin this year. Saw Jen. She's playing at the coffee shop on Fridays. Everyone else was normal. Fine." I'm telling the truth. It was a fine day. A normal day. The other kids said hello if they knew me before, and nothing to me if we'd never said hello before. No one asked how I was, and I'm happy for that. I want to believe that in Alaska, these kids are used to death. They hunt, they fish.

And maybe some haven't even heard. It's natural that Steven isn't there this year. He was a year older than I was and would be gone anyway. He'd be starting a brand-new life in college. But he hadn't been planning to do that. He'd been planning a new life, but not like the others. He had planned to do what most native Alaskans wouldn't even think of doing. Mostly it was people from the Lower 48 who tried it, people with a romantic idea of giving it all up. Shaking off custom, societies, expectations, to live a simple life in the interior, in the bush.

Those people go into the bush one summer; they build a shack and fish the river. They hunt moose, and salt and dry the meat. They dig a hole in the tundra for their freezer while the days are long and the sun bright. And they're living a very romantic life, but what they'll find out when winter hits is what native Alaskans already know. The winter might kill you, but the loneliness and the darkness will drive you crazy.

Steven knew this and had been preparing. Before me, he'd gone for weeks into the bush. He'd spent all winter break one year in a cabin he'd built in Chinitna Bay. He'd hired a floatplane to take all of his supplies. There was only a hermit who lived nearby, but he never saw him. Steven knew the hermit was alive because he found bundles of firewood missing. He stayed there through the snow, and winter solstice, and came out three weeks later.

"It was intense," he said. "I listened to my CB. I was talking to a guy in Russia. He didn't speak much English, and so sometimes, he'd just speak Russian, and I'd listen. I didn't know what he was saying. He could have said he wanted to fillet me and eat me for dinner, but just hearing him talk made me feel better."

Steven had been planning to spend the summer with me, and when I went back to school, he was going to move over to the bay and live off the land. His mom would let him because she was born in the bush. Her parents homeschooled her, and a teacher flew in once a year to assess the kids.

"I'd never seen running water until I was four and we flew out to my grandmother's funeral. I hadn't seen a car or even other little kids except in drawings in books. I hadn't seen stairs or a house with more than one room," she said. She often called driving into Homer "going to the city."

He took me to the cabin that last weekend we were together. We'd planned the trip for months. He wanted to see if I could make it out there.

"I need to know if you'll love me even after we haven't showered in days. I think it'll be the same as our time together in Homer. But I want to make sure," he'd said when he first asked me to go. "Plus I know you'll be turned on after watching me split wood."

"I've seen you split wood here," I said, thinking of times before we knew each other. Spring days when a glint of metal caught my eye through the fireweed and it was Steven chopping logs. One smooth drop, and the wood split and fell; the ax rose and another smooth drop.

"Yeah, but never after I haven't showered. Now, I know you can't resist that."

"Probably not."

I had never thought about living like that, but the cabin was homey. A heavy quilt covered the bed, and a black woodstove gave heat. In the night, the cabin was silent. There was no electricity and no buzz, which I realized all houses have. I was thinking I could live there too, but now I never want to cross the bay again. I can't fly in a floatplane, I can't live without that buzz that tells me I am not alone. There is someone connected to me somewhere.

Mom puts dinner in front of us. It's Gwen's favorite meal—pork chops and macaroni and cheese—though I remember a time it was mine, and later Dottie's. We sit, and Mom smiles at each of us.

"I'm glad we're all here," she says. Her pale skin is clear, and she's wearing a crisp white shirt. She looks like she should work at an office instead of a road construction site. But I know she loves what she does. The best thing about it, she always says, is that the women drive all the heavy machines—the roller and Ditch Witch—while the men, if there are any, hold the flags, standing in the road directing traffic.

"Me too," says Gwen. Dottie is chewing.

"Me three," I say.

The girls go into the living room and I hear Dottie ask Gwen to brush her hair.

"No way," says Gwen.

"Yes way," says Dottie.

"Leave her alone," Mom yells. There's quiet in the living room. I know Dottie will not leave her alone and that Mom knows Gwen needs her hair brushed. Gwen doesn't brush her own hair—she thinks if she uses No More Tears, it will take the tangles out on its own. It hasn't worked so far. Her black curls are matted and tangled, and the ponytail she puts it in is the same one from the night before. The quiet holds, and we both know Dottie has Gwen pinned on the floor, a single dangle of spit hovering just inches from her face. If Gwen screams, Dottie will let it drop.

"Okay," I hear Gwen say.

"You're a mess, munchkin," says Dottie, and she begins to brush.

"Help me clean?" says Mom. I begin clearing the dishes and handing them to her to wash.

"The Carters called today."

"They're back?" I ask. The Carters are the owners of the movie theater. They've been on vacation, and because I'm the only other employee, they shut down the theater while they were away. They weren't supposed to be back for another few days.

"They came home early."

"Is everything okay?"

Mom begins washing the dishes in a sink full of soapy water.

"Depends on how you look at it."

I give her another dish and she sighs.

"Martha, they sold the theater."

I stop with a dish halfway between the table and the sink. The theater has had a For Sale sign on it since before I started working there nearly two years ago. The sign is weathered, the *For Sale* now a pale pink instead of the original bright red. It has lost one of the nails holding it up, and now it is tilted and nearly falling.

"Who'd buy it?" I ask. For so long, no one would. The Carters could barely pay my wages. No one was getting rich. The Carters had owned the theater since Mr. Carter's dad threw some seats he bought at a fire sale in Anchorage into a garage and called it a movie house.

"When they were in California, they met a woman. She's young. She has some money. She's been to Homer before, and they said she nearly jumped at the chance to buy it. They didn't tell her how long it was on the market, so you shouldn't mention it." Her sink is empty and so I hand her the dish I've been clutching. Macaroni and cheese has gotten under my nail.

"They called to tell me I was fired?"

"No, they called to say that they sold the theater and that you still have a job. Mr. Carter told the new girl you were getting paid a dollar more than you really are. The girl asked how you could survive with such a low wage, so she's giving you a quarter more than he told her."

"This is quite a way to offer me a raise."

"Marty, they're old. They want to drive their motor home and see their daughter in Colorado. Give them a break. They want you to come in tomorrow after school to meet the new person. When you're there, say congratulations."

Mom takes the plate from me. She dries her hands on her jeans, and puts her arm around me.

"I know it sucks. I know all this sucks. But you're a good girl. You're smart. You're doing great." She kisses the top of my head. She smells a bit like hot asphalt.

"I'll be happy for them tomorrow. Tonight, I'll stew."

"That's my girl," says Mom. "Get everyone in the car. I'm treating to ice cream."

•   •   •

And I do stew, though we are driving down to the spit, all four of us in Mom's truck, Gwen sitting half on Dottie, half on me. I gnash my teeth as much as I can, but the evening is hot, in the seventies, and the ice cream turns out to be a rich chocolate. Gwen spots a single bald eagle sitting on the sand, and we watch the spit rats fish from the fishing hole they've cut in the sand. Each fall the Department of Fish and Game fills the hole with salmon eggs so they'll hatch and give the people who live there in the summer something to eat.

"Food source," says Dottie.

"Spit rats," Mom says.

"Mainlanders," I say. Standing on the sand with a spinner reel and net fishing for salmon that's been stocked is not fishing.

"It's polluted," says Gwen. She's been going with her classmates' families to pick up trash on the beach every Sunday for nearly three months.

"You guys have school tomorrow. We should get home."

The sun is still high, the sky a pale blue. I check my watch. Nine o'clock.

"I'm drinking coffee now," says Gwen.

"All right, shortie, you can stay up later than the rest of us, but we're heading home and going to bed," says Mom. She picks Gwen up, hangs her upside down and carries her to the car. Gwen lets her arms dangle and sticks her tongue out at me and Dottie from around Mom's hip.

I look at Dottie. "Sean coming over tonight?"

"You scared him away after your little tantrum this morning."

"No tantrum. He seemed okay during lunch."

"He was scared you'd rip him a new one."

"Whatever. He can come over. I don't care. Mom won't care. If you love him, then have him come over. If you love him, you can hold his hand in public," I say.

"I'm not you," she says, and puts her arm out. She hugs her hair and pretends to make out with some invisible boy.

"That's not me either."

"Please," she says, and opens her eyes and drops her arms.

"Everything I know I learned from you."

"Then you know the best form of birth control is an aspirin pressed firmly between your knees."

"You're so pristine."

Dottie smacks my butt hard and chases me into the car. Gwen sits all on my lap and I bury my face in her neck. She smells like rain.


And another day passes at school, and again no one says anything to me. Fewer people say hello, but Mr. Martin calls on me to remind him what pages we were supposed to read last night.

"Chapter one," I say.

"Good one," he says, and nods. "Did you read it?"

"I did."

"So you'll be my go-to girl. If I mess something up, you just jump in."

"Okay," I say, and smile. I don't jump in, because he never gets anything wrong, but he looks at me sometimes, and I nod to tell him he's on the right track. I know what he's doing; it's something I'd do for Gwen if she was feeling bad. But it works, and I take notes in his class and I laugh when the other kids laugh. My day has gone well.

Sean is taking Dottie home. "Promise you won't make out in front of Gwen," I say as she climbs into Sean's truck.

"I think I can handle it," she says.

"Gwen will need a snack when she gets there. You should offer Sean a snack too."

"Thanks, Martha. I think I can manage feeding them. And if for some reason I forget how to put peanut butter on bread, I bet one of them can figure it out."

"Okay," I say, and close the door to Sean's truck. I climb into the Jeep, pop Dottie's CD out of the player and just listen to the hum of the tires on the road.

The theater doors are open and the For Sale sign is down. There's a darker patch on the paint where it used to hang, the wood around it bleached. New movies are up on the marquee, but it still reads "World's Best Popcorn," which it really is. We use real butter and we put it in the middle and then on the top. I know people who worked at the chocolate shop and the café and they always say they got sick of the food, but I've never gotten sick of the popcorn at the theater.

No one is selling tickets and no one is behind the snack counter. I pull back one of the heavy burgundy curtains and look into the theater. Dark, and empty.

"Hello?" I call.

"Up here, honey," Mrs. Carter yells from the projection booth.

I head up the stairs, and Mrs. Carter gives me a hug before I'm even in the booth. Mr. Carter is behind her.

"We missed you," she says. "I got you a gift." She digs around in her bag.

"She got you something you'll never need or use," Mr. Carter says, and gives me a hug too. He smells like the cigars he sneaks when his wife isn't around.

Mrs. Carter hands me a snow globe, except there isn't any snow, just a plastic carrot and some tiny buttons. *Christmas in California* is printed around the base.

"Get it, honey? They don't have snow."

"I think it's cute," says a woman sitting behind the projector. On her finger she has the yellow tape we use to splice the film together.

Mom was right, she is young. She wears a T-shirt with Japanese cartoon characters on the front. Her jeans are a midnight blue, not the standard blue of preshrunk Levi's we buy at Homer's Jeans. Her hair is dyed a deep black, but a single gray streak runs down one side.

She stands and leans over to shake my hand, and so I take hers and press hard and look right into her eyes.

"Katherine Pine. I think I own this place." She raises her eyebrows, and I think, Dottie would die for eyebrows that naturally arched.

"Martha Powers. I hope I still work here."

"Believe me, you still do. You have a lot of teaching to do."

"We've been working on the place all day," says Mrs. Carter. "She's a quick study."

"Thanks, but I know I'm in need of an expert," says Katherine Pine.

"Marty's the one," says Mr. Carter. "Now, girls, I'm tired, and I don't have to be here, so we're leaving. Don't burn the place down and don't run my dad's business into the ground."

Katherine shakes his hand and both Carters give me another hug.

"Thanks for the snow globe."

"Do you really get it?" asks Mrs. Carter into my hair.

"I do," I whisper back.

We walk them down and say goodbye. I close the door and Katherine sits on the snack counter.

"Can you believe I bought a movie theater? In Alaska, no less." Her eyes are wide and she has her pale hand spread out on the legs of her dark jeans.

"I suppose it must be strange," I say.

"It was a little impulsive. But what the hell. Can we have some popcorn? Are there special bags for employees?"

"We just use lunch bags." I fill one with popcorn, butter and all, thinking she won't take it, or she'll wash it down with a diet soda. But she goes for the regular cherry soda.

"I had a boyfriend who worked at a movie theater in San Francisco. They had special bags. Inventory, so they could make sure no one was stealing. You don't steal, do you?"

"I try not to," I say.

She nods and looks around. "When was the last time the walls were painted?"

I didn't notice before, but the walls are a dingy white. Too many buttery hands, too many winters and leaks and mud.

"Before I started."

"Probably before talkies."

I nod again, but I'm sad. In my heart the theater is more than these ugly walls. It is where my mom took me for my first Disney movie. It is the first place my mom dropped me off alone. And it holds Steven.

We sat in the last row and kissed during a romantic comedy starring very good-looking people. It was an afternoon showing in the middle of winter, three o'clock and the sun had nearly set. We left the lights out and kissed more as the film ran down.

Katherine and I eat some popcorn. She looks around and shakes her head, then smiles and shakes her head some more.

"I was here once before. I came with my ex-husband last summer. We watched a movie about this secret agent. He goes to Paris and kills some people who are trying to kill him."

Steven and I saw that movie too. We sat in the first row, our heads back and my feet on his knees.

"We need to go to Paris. I want to see the *Mona Lisa,* but I hear it isn't that great," he said.

I'd never thought of going to Paris, but when Steven said that, it was all I had ever wished for.

"I remember that one," I say, and smile. "Cool car chase."

"Very cool. My husband didn't like it. He didn't like Alaska; he said it was too cold. It was sunny every day. He said the town bored him. What an ass. I knew it was over. You know what I mean? They can be such dicks."

"I don't have a husband, so I wouldn't know."

"Don't worry about the husband part. I'll get the grown-up advising stuff out of the way right now. Don't get married. And if you do, save your own money. Squirrel it away. And one day, when you want to be alone, you can have your own theater in Alaska."

"Advice taken."

"Good, and there will be no more. But you don't have a boyfriend at least?"

The Carters didn't tell her about Steven. And because they didn't, I want to tell her yes, that I have a wonderful boyfriend, with blue eyes like glacier water. He can shoot a caribou from three hundred yards. He fixes my Jeep when it breaks down and he burns me CDs with the saddest, loveliest music you've ever heard. And you probably haven't because he spends hours researching each artist. And he believes that there are many beautiful things I do, even though there aren't. This guy is my boyfriend and no one else's. Can you believe that? I want to ask, which is how I felt when Steven was alive.

But he isn't and she doesn't know anything and so she doesn't stare like others do, just a moment too long. I'm new to her. I can tell her any story I want. She is my fresh start. I decide to tell the most basic truth.

"No," I say. But this doesn't feel right either. I'm not a girl who is available for another boyfriend, not a girl who is looking. I still feel very taken. And if there is a boy who is even half as great as Steven was, we live in a small town, and there's no way that a boy would want to go out with me now.

"What do they say about the Alaska men? The odds are

good, but the goods are odd." She jumps off the counter. "I haven't finished splicing the new movie. I thought I would cry taping together all those previews. Any advice?"

"I can show you how I do it." To her, I am innocent, and I'm so grateful to her, for being new. For being an outsider too.

"Perfect." And we go into the projection booth and I take the metal reels, cool in my palms, and teach her how to splice the reel. The reels are just twenty minutes long and we have to tape the frames together so no one needs to sit back here the whole movie and flip reels.

"I can't believe I never noticed that the movies skip," she says, holding film up to the light.

"Film moves too fast for the human eye. We're actually watching two frames of the same image in a row. You never notice, do you?"

She shakes her head. "You'd think the owner of a movie house would know this kind of stuff."

"You're learning."

We finish splicing and I show her how to thread the projector. When we're done, she flicks the switch and the movie starts.

"We don't need to watch it," I say.

"But we can." She raises her eyebrows and puts her arm through mine. She grabs more popcorn for me and some for herself and she sits us in the middle row, middle seats.

"I've never sat here," I say. I normally choose an aisle seat so I can get up if I want. When Steven was here, he would pick a spot up close, or someplace just far enough away from others. And sometimes, he'd just pause in a row and plop down, even if it meant he was staring at the back of a head.

"My mom always sits in the middle, so I do too. Is it strange?" she whispers, though we are the only ones in the theater.

"No," I whisper back. "I like it." I do. And I sit and watch the movie and it's perfect. I don't have to lean to catch something at the edge of the screen. I'm not too close that my neck gets sore. I'm in a new place, a place free for a moment from my mother, and from Steven, and before I realize he is gone from me, I am happy.


Mom's home when I get there. The girls are fed and doing homework at the table, though I see Dottie has a letter addressed to Sean, and Gwen is using her pen to trace her cuts on a photograph of a frog.

"What's she like?" Mom asks. She sits at the table, her hands pressed between her knees.

"Who?" I ask, though I know.

"The new girl. The owner."

"She's definitely from California. Her hair is dyed. She wore a cool T-shirt. She's nice and funny."

"Not too bright though," says Mom.

"She's very smart. She caught on right away."

"Well, she's not smart enough to avoid making rash, probably terrible business decisions."

I shrug and pull a plate from the refrigerator. I don't want to talk about Katherine like that.

"Why'd she buy a movie theater in Homer, Alaska?"

"She had some money saved," I say.

"But why Alaska?"

"The beauty," I say, because that's what everyone who comes here from somewhere else would say.

The next day we open after two weeks of being closed. Katherine has dressed the part of an Alaskan. She wears faded jeans and a plain T-shirt and a bandanna covering her hair. I am disappointed for a moment that she isn't wearing her Japanese T-shirt, but as I look closer, I see her jeans are designer and instead of sneakers or hiking boots she wears black leather boots with a tall heel. I wish she'd take off her bandanna and show her hair, that bright gray streak glowing almost white. People might look for an extra second, but we're forgiving in this town. There's a man who dresses like a woman, and a whole lot of women who dress and act like men.

The theater smells like the first day of school, and I find a wet mop in the supply cabinet. The bathrooms are immaculate and there are fresh flowers behind the ticket counter. There is also a fresh schedule of new movies. Two action movies and a coming-of-age story about a New Zealand girl. When you're the only movie theater in town, people like whatever you put in front of them.

Tonight is the movie I watched with Katherine last night. It is a lovely movie about a boy, a smart boy, who plays chess. He wears glasses he doesn't need. He loves a girl and teaches her to play, but she is never any good, but he loves her still. And finally at the end he leaves his glasses off for good. It seems simple, but for me it is a true story. I believe in love. I believe in beauty. This movie is both.

People are lined up at the door and I recognize groups of kids from my school. Some of them are in my classes, and I begin to worry, not that they'll treat me just slightly strange like they do at school, but that somehow Katherine will find out about me. Maybe she'll be in the bathroom and hear one of the girls tell her friend she can't believe I can still work after everything. Maybe a boy will tell a story about the night the film broke and while I was in the booth madly cutting and taping, Steven stood in front of the audience and told jokes. They were terrible jokes. Jokes we'd all heard a million times. What's black and white and red all over? Knock knock. Who's there? Alaska. Alaska who? I'll ask ya later. But he told them and the audience shouted the answers back and laughed until the movie started again.

And if she hears, she'll be like everyone else. She'll be kind and will smile when she sees me, but I'll forever be different in her mind. I won't simply be the girl who runs the register. That's all I want to be anymore.

Katherine checks the cash in the register one last time. She scoops the popcorn again. She smacks her hands on her thighs.

"Are you ready for this? Because I don't think I am."

"You are," I say.

"Can we go through it one more time?"

"They tell you how many. You tell them how much. They give you money. Have you been to the movies before?"

"I have, smart-ass. Now, if you don't straighten up, I'll leave right now." She points the popcorn scoop at me.

"You'd love that. Just sit back and watch the money roll in."

"I'll fire myself, honest. Don't doubt me."

"You're ready, I'm ready. Open the doors."

She shakes the popcorn scoop at me one more time, sighs and shrugs. She walks to the doors after sticking her tongue out at me. There's a glint of silver in her mouth. She opens the door.

"Welcome," she says to a group of girls from my school. One of them helped on the whale a few days a week. Katherine takes their money and they check her out. I can tell they're trying to get a look at her hair beneath the bandanna. I can tell that I'll be at school next week and someone will walk in with a big skunk streak bleached into her hair.

They pass through and smile at me.

"Hey, Marty," a girl says. Her hair is nearly black and she'd be a good candidate for the bleach job. I don't know her name, and before this summer she hadn't known mine.

"Hey," I say, and smile. I act glad to see all of them, like they are more to me than just a few girls that I've passed in the halls.

Some people stare. The old women just pat my hand without ordering anything. Some couples, friends of Steven's mom, come in and say hello extra loud. They ask about school, and I wish they wouldn't. Katherine keeps looking over at me. I know she's just looking, worried that she's doing something wrong. But she isn't. It was me who did something wrong.


The line clears and Katherine shuts the register. She closes the doors and the curtains.

"We need a bottle of champagne," she says. I pour her some Seven-Up.

"Best of the bubbly," I say, and hold my cup to hers.

"Not to celebrate. I need some booze to calm my nerves."

"Root beer?"

"Come on, we have to start the movie," she says, and knocks her cup into mine. We run up the stairs. I've already threaded the movie for her. She smiles and looks out the window over the audience.

"You are all under my spell. You will love every movie we show. You will come again and again and bring your friends."

"Abracadabra and amen," I say. "Now start it."

She flips the sound and turns on the projector. Katherine claps and hugs me. "We're in business!" she says. And we are.

"But we'll be out of business if we don't head down."

"Okay." She follows me out of the booth and back down the stairs. "Can I peek in?"

"No," I say. "You'll let light in, and plus you didn't pay."

"How about I sign your paycheck and you let me peek?"

"After the previews when everyone is settled. It looks better then."

And so she waits patiently, and I'm proud of her.

"You did a good job," I say. She pauses with popcorn halfway to her mouth.

"Thanks, Martha. You did a great job." She smiles and eats the popcorn. Maybe this is the moment to ask her why she would do something as crazy as leave California to buy a movie theater in Alaska. But then she might ask why everyone talks so loudly to me, or not at all. She might ask why I pause each time at the curtain, bracing myself to go into the theater, trying to prepare myself for another moment that he is here and not here at the same time.

Katherine pokes her head in when I tell her she can. I look around the other curtain, and they're sitting there like they always do. Some lean in to the person next to them. Some raise popcorn to their mouths. The theater is dark and I see a beam of light from Katherine's curtain. I should tell her to shut it, but I can imagine how these people must look to her. They look content, safe and warm. And she has given this to them. So I let her peek and allow a single shaft of light into the dark theater. Eventually the thrill will wear off.

The movie ends and Katherine stands at the door, saying goodbye to each person. She is smiling, her lips red with a deep crimson lipstick. With the sunlight washing over her pale skin, she looks like she could be one of the stars from that film. She is elegant, young and cool. The girls pause next to her and say goodbye back.

"Thank you for coming," she says, and nods.

"Thank you for having us," says a girl in my computer class. I think she might just curtsy and then I would gag for sure. But her friend pushes her, eager for her moment with Katherine.

Some of the adults introduce themselves, and the men Katherine's age pull at their flannel shirts, hands covering holes torn from fishing hooks or too many washes. Katherine thanks them and nods once for each person.

When they're all gone, I grab the broom to sweep the popcorn and crumpled cups. Katherine grabs a broom too.

"One sec," she says, and runs up to the booth. I hear her up there rattling the reels, and for a second the projector flips on. She cusses.

"Need some help?" I call.

"I'm ignoring you," she says. "Got it." She takes the steps two at a time and bursts through the curtain just as Madonna tells me I can dance.

"For inspiration," Katherine calls out with Madonna.

"You're kidding," I say, laughing.

"I know she isn't as popular with the young folk like you. But for an old lady like me, she is the voice of a generation."

"And how does 'Like a Virgin' represent your generation?" I ask. Katherine is singing into the top of her broom. She knows all the words.

"You're too mature to understand," she shouts to the beat of the song. She dances in the aisles and keeps singing into the broom. She points at me and shakes her hips. And so I start to dance too. I know some of the words and so we both sing, shouting more than anything, like Gwen does when she sings to the oldies station.

We dance until the song ends, and the next is a ballad. Katherine knows the words to that song too. She begins to sweep and so do I, but I wouldn't mind dancing again.

When we are done, she turns out the lights. The sun is setting, though it is past ten.

"They think I'm not cut out for this," she says as she locks the door.

"Who and cut out for what?" Though I know.

"These people. They think I'm here on a lark. They think I'm just a stupid California girl."

"Katherine, everyone here is a bit stupid. Why would anyone choose to live here? It snows, there's no sunlight in winter. If anything, I think they wonder why you left California."

"I left for the same reasons anyone leaves a place. For a new start. To find new people. I wanted new friends and sights. I wanted to not be reminded that I had been married, or that I shopped at a certain store. I was tired of being defined." She shakes the door. It's locked. It's a truthful answer. After she shakes the door once more, harder than needed, I realize that's the last time I'll get to ask.

"Some people have never left here," I say.

"Because they know that this place is so much better than anyplace else."

"How would they know that if they've never left?"

"I'm telling you, I've traveled all over," she says. "I've seen a lot of big cities and small towns, and this place is the best. The people here must have a sixth sense."

"No, they just don't leave."

"When you leave, you'll see what I mean."

I shake my head. I want nothing more than to leave, to go away and never come back. But I know she's right. I have what I need here, and if I left, it would be to find Steven. To make things right. And there's no place I can ever do that.

"Good job," she says when we reach my car.

"Good job."

"See you tomorrow." She walks toward a truck I recognize from the parking lot at my school. She must have bought it from the kid when he went away to college.

"Not if I see you first." I wave and pull out of the parking lot. I drive, and there is fog across the bay, but Iliamna's peak has broken through. Sunlight shines through that one patch, and it's true, and I'm a bit disappointed: there really is no more beautiful place than the one I am in right at this moment.

I wait until even Dottie is asleep. She's been out three nights in a row with Sean, and I know she's tired. No amount of concealer can cover the dark circles under her eyes, but she's happy and her cheeks are rosy. So after the sun has gone down and the night is dark, but still a glowing blue, I leave my house. I walk down the road and as I'm halfway there, the wind begins to blow. I look to the bay. Heavy clouds cover the mountains. There the sky holds deep black rain clouds. It takes a few hours, but the weather will make it here, and with the winds blowing it will come faster. I rush to his house.

I climb in through the same window, and instead of lying in the front room, I go to Steven's bedroom. I lay my sleeping bag out where his bed was, and from here all I can see is sky, and the clouds blowing past in the wind. I watch them and wait. Steven and I spent one night in his room when his mother and brother went on a field trip in Anchorage.

"I have a surprise for you," he said at school that day. "Come over when everyone has gone to bed. Come over hungry."

At home that night, I pushed my dinner around and then I studied until everyone had gone to sleep.

I knocked at his window, and I found the lights on beneath the blinds.

"Marty," he called to me from the front door. I jumped.

He let me in. Candles burned, and the house smelled like garlic and fresh bread. Pots were on the stove and pans and bowls were in the sink.

"I made you dinner," he said. Spaghetti and sauce from scratch and garlic bread and salad. It was all set out on the table, candles lit and napkins folded.

"My mom and my brother are gone. We have the place to ourselves. I wanted to play house with you."

"It's beautiful. Thank you," I said as he pulled a chair out for me.

He kissed my neck and I felt his skin, smoother than mine would ever be.

"I wanted it to be perfect for you." And I know that he did, and when he sat across from me, he smiled. It reminded me of a movie we showed at the theater, *Sixteen Candles.* At the end, sitting in the theater, I'd wished someone would make a table very beautiful just for me.

Steven had done that, but it was better because it was him. This very beautiful boy.

"Thank you," I said again.

"You're welcome," he said, and we ate. And we didn't clean up; instead, we went to his room. The room I am in right now. And we spent the night in a proper bed. His sheets were flannel with salmon on them. His comforter was down. It was a twin bed and so we were close all night. He smelled like the outside, of pine and sap and grass. And we slept until just before sunrise, when I woke up. It was much earlier than I had set the alarm for.

He slept quietly, but his eyes were squinted like Dottie's are when she doesn't want me to know she's awake.

"Are you awake?" I asked, but he still slept, his breathing deep and steady.

"Steven, wake up."

His eyes opened. He blinked once and focused on me.

"What's up?" he said.

"I realized it was stupid to sleep when we have this whole house together."

He rubbed his eyes and stretched. "You're right," he said. He held me and kissed my cheeks and my lips and my stomach and later we cleaned the kitchen. Our hands in soapy water, a CD he called the beauty CD playing over the speakers as the sun rose. The sky burned red and gold and for one night I knew what it was like to live with him, to play house, as he said. I cried as he walked me home. I cried as I kissed him goodbye. I cried and I didn't care that Dottie and Gwen saw me walk in through the front door. Mom was gone, but I don't think she would have asked where I'd been either.

So now I lie in his cold room and if I turn my head I can still smell trees and cut grass. And here are the things I know: Time will never be what my watch says. Time passes too fast when you just want it to stop, and time passes too slow when all you wish for is a lifetime in a minute. It'll just never be what it really is, hands moving over a clock. And then the rain starts.

• • •

It's a few days later and Katherine has stopped greeting every person who walks through the door. Today she has a pattern: she says hello to every third person, and nods so the second person feels like he or she has been greeted first. She's less nervous and I'm relaxing at each showing as well. People are stopping to chat with her about the weather or the moose hunt. She nods more and smiles and sometimes winks at me when they leave. But people still treat me the same. And she hasn't noticed.

Everyone's settled in the theater. The projector is running, Katherine is reading the local paper and I'm studying for Mr. Martin's class. I've been answering questions in his class. I don't raise my hand, but somehow when I know the answer he knows to call on me. The first time I was scared. I gave my answer and class went on as usual. I picked up my pen, ready to take notes, but my heart was beating and my hands were shaking so badly, I couldn't concentrate. Instead I looked out at the browning trees, more going every day.

"Mother nature is in charge," said the arborist who came to science class. It's okay, because the cottonwoods will take over, and some of the conifers will survive, and they'll spread again. They'll be stronger, and the lumber people can take them without cutting anything else down, but still, looking out at those dead trees saddens me. I'm sure there's something that can be done. But maybe not. Who am I to say?

"Hey, Martha, you're a native Alaskan, right?" Katherine says, looking up from her paper.

"Born in Anchorage."

"You fish, right?"

"I do."

"Can you clean a caribou?"

"Probably. Do you have one waiting behind the soda machine?"

"Can you change your oil?"

"That I leave to my sister's boyfriend."

Katherine folds the paper. She leans back, her arms crossed.

"I want to do that."

"Change your oil? I can ask Sean to do it for you. If you let them into a movie, he'd do it for free."

"They can come in whenever they want, family is free. I want to fish. I want to hunt. I want to be an Alaska girl."

I close my book and fold my arms and look at her like she's looking at me.

"We can fish whenever you want. As for hunting caribou, that's sitting in a blind for days on end, and most people never even shoot one. You can't get out, or they'll scent you. You have to pee in a can. And it's not the season."

"I'm not ready to pee in a can," she says. "But I'm ready to fish."

"Okay," I say. "We have to do it on the weekend. We have to get up early. It's strictly catch and release. The fish are spawned out and not good tasting."

"See? I want to know that sort of thing."

"Well, I'm telling you."

"I'll do whatever you tell me."

"Sunday we'll go. I'll drive. You need felt-bottomed waders, a fishing license and long underwear. I'll provide the fly poles and hooks. I'll pick you up at five. That's A.M. Got it?"

"Yes, master. My goodness, a California girl wants to fish and suddenly it's brain surgery."

"Do you want to fish?"

"I do," she says, and goes back to her paper. I go back to my book, but I'm excited to show Katherine something. I'm excited to fish. I haven't been all summer. I hate to think of all the things I haven't done this summer.

I drive home listening to a CD Steven made me. It is the second one he made; the first was a Christmas gift. We weren't yet going out, but I missed him much more than I should have when he didn't show up at the whale for a day. I thought he made CDs for all of his friends for Christmas, and so when he gave me the first one, I was flattered.

"Thank you," I said. "I don't really have anything for you." I had wanted to get him many things. A cool buck knife I'd seen, fishing lures and a book on tying flies. I'd spent hours at the hardware store touching hunting and camping equipment, but I never got him anything. I thought if I did it would mean I liked him more than I thought I did, but in truth, just spending so much thought on him should have told me.

"No need to get me anything." He smiled at me. And so I hugged him. It was the first time I'd been that close to him and he was warm, soft and strong. He smelled green, like Alaska will always smell to me. He hugged me back, cleared his throat.

"You're very welcome."

And that first CD is wonderful. There is a man with his

guitar singing softly about a parade. And there is a song about time, time revealing who the woman singing really is, about how it will reveal us all. When I first listened, I thought he put these songs on each person's CD.

I listen to that CD when I miss him. But as I drive home and try to remember all of the secret coves, the king salmon holes, the flies and how to cast with each pattern, I miss him terribly. He always knew the right weight so the hook would just bounce along the bottom.

I rev the engine and go too fast, but I'm in control and the CD is on loud. The second CD is faster. The first time I listened to it, I thought he was mad at me, but as I listened closer I knew he was mad at himself. There are songs about secrets, and a boy who is only half right. The day he gave me the CD, he hadn't been at the whale and I was disappointed. I walked to my car, searching the lot for his truck, hoping he was just late. I didn't see his truck, but I found him waiting at my Jeep. His cheeks were red, the wind whipping us both.

"I made you another CD. I wanted to give it to you."

"You didn't have to," I said. I took it and hoped he didn't see my hands shaking.

"I did. I spent a long time on it."

"Thank you, again. The first one was beautiful."

He leaned over and kissed my cheek and his skin was so cold I felt my own nearly burn him. He pulled back and I leaned in farther, but he was stepping back.

"See you tomorrow." He turned and left.

And so I listened carefully to that CD, and after the first two times I hoped the songs were truly for me. I couldn't believe they were.

The next day I caught him in the hall.

"I listened to it. A few times."

"Good," he said. "I'm glad you like it."

"I like it very much. I can tell you spent a long time making it."

"I did." A bell rang for us to get to class. We had one minute.

"Steven," I said. A kid ran past me, his backpack grazing my arm. I took a breath. "I hope those songs are about me."

"They are," he said. He kissed me once on my mouth and turned and ran to class. I stood in the hall, fingers to my lips, believing every word of every song he had given me.

Gravel kicks up behind my tires as I turn onto our road. Clumps of mud hit the wheel wells and I skid into our driveway with the music blaring, and my ears are ringing. My skin is cold like his was the afternoon he gave me the CD.

Dottie runs out the front door.

"Hey, Teen Angst, turn the music down," she hollers, running down the stairs.

"Hey, Dottie, I need your expertise on Sunday."

"Hey, Marty, I need you to focus for one second right now."

"I'm taking Katherine fishing. I haven't been since last year. Where should we go?"

"Walk the Russian River for trout. Salmon, go to the Kenai Reserve. Catch and release only." She's opened my door before I even have my seat belt off.

"Thanks, sis. Such service. What fly pattern?"

"Marty. You're dense. Use an egg pattern for trout, streamers or wet flies for salmon. Now, I've told you what you need to know. Brace yourself."

I hop out of the Jeep and nearly land on her toe.

"What, Maybelline has just come out with the perfect pink? Not too rosy, not too purple. Like freshly kissed lips . . ."

"That would be awesome, but this isn't good news." Her cheeks are pink, no makeup, and her hazel eyes are a bright yellow like they turned when she had a fever.

"Are you sick?"

"I'm not sick. Worse. Dad's in there."

"In the house? Where's his car?"

"I don't know. Mom picked him up from the ship. He's back on leave."

He checks the weather stations along the whole coast of Alaska for the Coast Guard. He goes for months at a time. I picture him out there in the wind, icicles on his eyebrows and nodding to another man, a thermometer in his hand. "Yep, it's cold."

It's ridiculous, and he's ridiculous. He normally lives in Fairbanks, but sometimes he decides he wants to see his family. But only sometimes. And never when we need him.

My parents aren't married, and they never were. Though when I was born they lived together. He took the Coast Guard job just after Dottie was born. And as for Gwen, I can only guess that my mother wanted another child. I believe she knew that we needed another girl here, to even out the numbers. And that she loves my father, and only him, because he is the only man who ever spends the night. Though every time, he's gone before we wake.

"He's not staying here," I say, closing my door as quietly as I can, but I'm sure he knows I'm home.

"I don't know what the hell is going on. Don't worry." Dottie bites her lips. She grabs my hand; hers are clammy.

"It's okay," I say, though I'm glad everyone knows what can and can't be told. He knows Steven is gone, but he doesn't know how. He doesn't know I was there.

Dad was on the ship when it happened. Mom called him to say that my boyfriend had died.

"I'm sorry," he said after he asked to speak to me.

"We all are," I said, and after that there was silence.

"He was a good boy."

"He was," I said, though my dad hadn't met him. He was never around when Steven was in my life, and I doubt I would have introduced them. Steven was too skinny for my dad's tastes. Steven was too quiet and my dad would have called him a mainlander behind his back. He would never believe me if I told him that Steven could have survived months longer in the bush than he could.

More quiet on the line, and finally I said, "Goodbye."

"Bye," he said, and we both hung up.

"Are you ready?" Dottie asks, and we walk up the stairs hand in hand.

"Never."

"It's okay, neither is he."

"Let's make it quick."

She opens the door and there he is. My dad. He wears a flannel shirt and jeans. The Alaska man's uniform. His face is tan and his eyes are bright yellow like Dottie's. And for a moment all of our features fall and scatter and rearrange themselves on him. He gave Gwen her nose, thin and turned up just slightly at the tip. And I have his smile—broad, too many teeth showing. And all of our traits combine to make him look very proper. He looks like he should have a yellow sweater draped over his shoulders and crisp tennis whites beneath.

"Hey, Madge," he says.

"Hey, Dad," I say, and hug him. Mom raises her eyebrows at me behind his back. She shrugs once and rolls her eyes.

"How are you doing?" He bows his head a bit to look, I'm sure he thinks, deeply into my eyes.

"Good, school's good. Work's good. We have a movie I don't mind watching a million times."

"How are you really doing? I bet you miss that boy." He's still staring at me. And I close my eyes. When I was a kid my dad once told me that if I can't see someone, chances are they can't see me either. And I wish that trick always worked, but when I open my eyes he is still there waiting for the answer.

"His name was Steven. I miss him very much." I stare back. I stare without blinking. He looks away first and I've won that small round.

"I heard the theater was bought. I heard she's just a girl."

"She's not eight," Mom calls out from the table, shaking a pizza box.

"She's actually twenty-eight," I say. "She's from California."

"Why buy a movie theater? Where'd she get the money?"

"She won the lottery. She blackmailed her lover. She's

really a hit man, and this is a cover," I say. I peel cheese from the pizza box, then take a seat as Mom hands me a plate.

"She's a bank robber," Gwen shouts from the couch, where she's reading a book with dragons on the cover. I wink at her. Instead of winking she blinks both eyes and turns her head so I can see just one eye.

"She's a supermodel," says Dottie.

"Highly probable," I say.

"Anyway," my dad says, and sits at the table. Mom has her chin in her palm. If it were anyone else, she would tell us to quit. But she watches us volley back and forth, a half smile on her lips.

"I personally think she is the plastic surgeon to the stars," Mom says. They've already eaten, and Mom picks up her plate and my dad's plate and takes them to the sink.

"I believe all of you. She must be quite a girl." My dad leans back in his chair, raises his arms above his head and stretches.

"I'm taking her fishing," I say before my mother turns around. I know that if nothing else, my dad loves to fish. It's where Dottie got her instinct.

"Where are you going?"

"Kenai. We're going Sunday morning. Cooper Landing, I think."

"Good choice. But it will be serious combat fishing there. You'll have to hike upstream a ways. Get away from the parking lot. You want salmon, trout, dollies—what are you looking for?"

"Salmon. Sockeyes," I say. With their emerald faces and ruby red bodies, these salmon seem almost unnatural in their beauty.

"Get your fly rod and flies," he says, and so we are set for the night. He holds me hostage tying flies and assembling rods. He describes a cloudy day and a sunny day and which angle to stand in each. Gwen reads and Dottie sits with us, tying the flies Dad shouts out to her. She ties pink floozies, dry mosquito flies, egg patterns and emerging patterns—Gwen calls them half-bugs because they're halfway between a larva and an insect. With each fly, he leaves a note with how, where and when to cast.

Dottie sits close to me while he describes some finer element of a fly rod versus a spinner reel. Her tongue sticks out of her mouth as she winds thread around a tiny hook. She squints, and when she's done she smiles at the bit of fluff and beads and metal. She puts it down and smiles again, and because my sister is happy, I am happy. This is why it's good that he still comes around, even if it is just every once in a while.

In the morning we wake and he is gone, the sheets folded at the foot of the couch. Mom is gone too. And again it is the three of us. The three sisters.


After school the next day, I catch Mom in the kitchen.

"What was that all about? Why was he here?"

"Just here," she says. Her back is to me as she scrubs a mug that's already clean.

"Did you know he was coming?"

"I hoped," she says, turning off the water. She dries her hands on a towel and smiles at me. "It's okay to miss people."

"I know, Mom. It's just weird to find him here. It stresses Dottie out. And me."

"He's your dad. It's good for you girls to see him. To re-member you have a dad."

"I don't forget, but I think he does."

"He doesn't. He just knows his girls are pretty inde-pendent. He likes to know that we're able to keep ourselves together without his help. Makes him proud."

I roll my eyes. "Yeah, right," I say, though it's true. I wouldn't want him around all the time anyway. We girls get along just fine.

It's Friday night. Katherine wears her tall boots and a black sweater with a boatneck. Her lips are the same dark matte red from her first day at the theater, and the streak in her hair shines white.

"Date night," I say.

"Will you be mine?" she asks, her hands over her heart.

"Maybe we can go see a movie." I bat my eyelashes at her.

People are lined up outside. We begin letting them in, and already I notice more red lipstick on the girls from my school. I take their tickets and Katherine scoops popcorn and hands out drinks. More people are talking to her, and she's better with them.

"Rain coming," she says to the old man who owned the original parcel of land my house and Steven's house sit on.

"Looks like," he says, and takes a bag of popcorn.

"I have some extra peas from my greenhouse, if you'd care for some," says the woman who works at the library.

"Sounds wonderful. Thank you." Katherine smiles and nods.

Dottie and Sean come down the line. Sean has his wallet out.

"Hey, kids," I say. "This is a family theater. We don't want your kind here."

Dottie nudges Sean and he hands me some money.

"Two, please," he says.

"I got you this time." I push his money back at him.

"Is that her?" Dottie whispers as she leans over the ticket counter. She nods in Katherine's direction.

"Who do you think it is?" I whisper back, leaning close to her, our noses practically touching. She flinches and moves back.

"You know."

"The queen of Sheba?"

"Yeah," Dottie says.

"I guess so." I lean back and sell another ticket. Dottie is holding up the line. She moves and Katherine says hello.

"That's my sister and her boyfriend," I say extra loud. Sean looks away, but Dottie straightens up.

"Pleasure to meet you," Dottie says, and I want to roll my eyes, but for Dottie this is a big moment. A real Californian is in our midst, and I'm sure to Dottie, Katherine does look like the queen of Sheba.

"The pleasure is mine." Katherine bows. She hands them a bag of popcorn and waves Sean's money away. "Consider it bribery. Just in case your sister deserts me I need someone to run the joint."

"Will do," says Dottie. Sean puts his hand on the small of her back and holds the curtain as they walk into the theater.

Soon the line dies and it's just me and Katherine again.

She starts the movie and comes back down. We begin our routine of cleaning and sweeping. She counts out the ticket register.

"Why no date tonight?" she asks me.

"Same reason you're hanging out at a movie theater with a seventeen-year-old."

"You consider men a disease too?"

I scrub at a spot on the counter. It's a spot I've scrubbed a number of times, and I know it won't come up, but I can't look at her.

"You sure are bashful right now. Is there a boy?" She looks at me through narrowed eyes.

I stop scrubbing and look up at her. I breathe. Inhale and exhale. The tears are gone, I say to myself, trying to stop them. But my eyes are already clouding over. Katherine's smile fades. She drops the cash into the register and slams it shut.

She comes behind my counter, and just as the tears spill over she puts her arms around me. She rocks me side to side and I cry hot tears into her black sweater.

"I'm sorry," she says into my hair. "I'm so sorry."

She hands me a napkin and takes another and presses it to my eyes.

"What is it?" she asks, but that makes me cry harder. I feel like such an idiot, standing behind the snack counter crying my eyes out. But my feet are cemented to the ground, my knees locked in place, like they were that afternoon across the bay with him. I can't move. I can only stand and stare. I see nothing, and I see myself all at the same time. I see a girl who can't move.

Something cool is pressed to my forehead and my vision returns. Katherine has her hand on my head, a wet napkin between our skin.

"I'm okay," I say.

"Okay."

A little boy in cowboy boots runs into the lobby from the theater. He's bobbing from one foot to the other.

"Next to the stairs," Katherine calls, and points to the bathroom. He runs to the door and disappears inside.

"Martha, what did I do?"

"You didn't do anything."

"Is it that all boys are bad, or just one in particular?"

"Neither."

"Okay," she says, and dabs at my face again. "Are you going to tell me?"

Her red lips are pressed together. She holds the crumpled-up napkin in her hand. Her hands are pale and small and her nails are painted dark purple, almost black. Her forehead is squished; she worries about me.

"Seriously, it takes a lot to shock me. I lived in San Francisco for nearly ten years. I grew up in L.A. Do you love girls and not boys? I'm cool with that. Did someone hit you? I'll hit him back. Does he love someone else? Well, that girl's a slut with bad shoes." She pours some Seven-Up and adds some grenadine. She hands it to me and I take a sip.

"We really need to get some liquor behind this counter," she says, and smiles. She takes the Shirley Temple and drinks some too. "This stuff isn't quite strong enough."

Another tear falls, the single drop spreading dark blue on the knee of my jeans. She presses the rough napkin to my face again and I really want to tell her. I even take a deep breath, ready to say it. She is watching me. But all I can manage is to take the cup back from her and sip some of the red cherry fizz. There just aren't words yet for what happened that afternoon.

"Okay," she says. "You'll tell me when you're ready. And until then I'll wonder. And I'll either kick every guy's ass that looks at you, or I'll hand him your work schedule and phone number."

"How about neither," I say. "There's nothing to be done." I leave the counter and go to the restroom to rinse my face. My skin is blotchy and my nose bright red. I splash more water on my face and breathe more and soon I am back to where I was before I cried. I am back to that very quiet place. A place quiet like the bottom of the ocean, dark and deep beneath the earth. I am all of those things, but I know this is not right either.

The movie ends and Dottie and Sean say good night. Dottie looks at me a second too long. My nose is still red, I'm sure.

"Allergic reaction," she says while Sean stands near.

"Shellfish, I think," I say.

She nods, knocks once on the glass counter. "Need anything?"

"No, I'll see you later."

They leave and when the theater is cleared out, Katherine sends me home.

"I can stay. I'll help clean."

"They were a neat bunch. That new 'Keep the Theater Clean' ad must be working."

"Okay," I say.

"Have a good night," she says, and hugs me.

And I drive straight home. I drive and watch the Anchor River. It's flowing from the rains, but trees form dams every few yards. More dead spruce from the beetle. The fish like the slow pools that collect at the bases of the dams. It gives them a resting place as they swim upstream to spawn, though fewer each year swim up the Anchor.

And on my way home I hear a single gunshot ricochet off the hills and the trees. I shudder once and ignore the echo that lingers in my ears.

I spend Saturday getting out waders, tying up poles, putting the roof on the Jeep. Dottie helps and Gwen plays outside in the fireweed. She plays Marco Polo, but there is no one she is playing with.

"Sometimes she scares me," says Dottie as Gwen hollers, "Marco."

"Polo," Gwen cries back in a deeper, boy's voice.

"It's just how she plays," I say, though seeing the fireweed part and my sister's black curls travel through the tall grass searching this way and that for an invisible friend, I agree with Dottie.

"We never played like that."

"We had each other. We have each other." Dottie and I are just under a year apart, but Gwen is nearly ten years younger than Dottie.

"Maybe we should give her more attention. We don't want her killing kittens or holding up gas stations."

"She's fine," I say. "She's from the same blood we are."

"That blood's done both of us a lot of good." Dottie goes back to biting a shot weight onto the line. She presses it between her fingers to make sure it will hold.

Gwen keeps calling out in the tall grass. I know I should stop her: Dottie is right. She should play like normal kids do. There are girls up the road her age. But she is happy chasing her echo with the purple fireweed flowers catching and tangling in her hair.

I make two coffees, milk and sugar, one for Katherine and one for me. It is early, the sun just risen and the sky purple, the clouds a deep gray. Rain today, I think, though as I drive to Katherine's there are pockets of clear sky and I really can't be sure what the day will bring.

When I get to her house, I'm impressed. It's a log house with huge diamond-shaped windows. It's set on a slight hill and she has a view of the spit, into the bay, and in the distance I see Mount Saint Augustine. She's renting from a couple who only come up for a week in the beginning of summer. She has to find a permanent place, but with the wildflowers in bloom in the front and logs a warm orange from being freshly treated, I wouldn't be looking too fast for a new home. Her dusty truck is in the drive, and before I can honk she steps out the front door and locks it behind her. She hasn't been living here that long. I can't think of the last time I locked our door.

She wears overalls and a fishing jacket still creased from the plastic it came in. Her cheeks are pink, and her blue eyes are pale. She's tired, but she waves and smiles as she sees me pull up. Her breath comes in puffs of white as she climbs in.

I hand her the coffee and she drinks deeply.

"Thanks," she says, and we drive. I've chosen a CD Steven made, all classical music. And this is a secret I didn't know until near the end when we went to Anchorage for the day to buy a water purifying system he'd been saving for. He touched my back and guided me away from the entrance of the outdoors store to a piano shop. He sat down at a bench in front of a glossy black piano and began playing endless notes, one piled on top of the other. He kept his eyes open and smiled and raised his eyebrows as he played, like he couldn't believe it either.

"My dad made sure I could play. I liked the lessons, surprisingly, and so I learned," he said, never missing a note.

"There's no piano in your house."

"I practice at school," he said.

I asked him to make me a CD of all the classical music he could play. And as I drive with Katherine, the sky turning a pale blue, we listen to all the music he'll never play for me.

"Moose," I say, pointing into a meadow filled with dwarf birch and pale green grass. There are two bulls knocking into each other but not seriously. Just the two of them, unless there is a female near that I don't see.

"Amazing," says Katherine. And I suppose it is.

We drive and I point out a magpie, the ravens, a porcupine flattened in the road.

"Poor thing," says Katherine.

"When she was a kid, Dottie thought they were cute

too. One night a little one came into the yard. Dottie saw him and ran out and you can guess the rest."

"I suppose you Alaska kids learn lessons the hard way."

We drive on and the clouds are breaking apart. It might end up being sunny.

"I'm thinking about having some independent films to show at the theater. Good ones, not boring or weird, but not always the same blockbuster crap. Any thoughts?"

My tires are humming on the road and I pass an RV going much too slow for my taste.

"As long as they're not weird, it sounds good. Sometimes we used to show old movies. Just for a night or two during the week. People liked that."

"I was thinking about that too. And I was thinking about couches. Take out some of the broken chairs, throw in a couch and a little coffee table."

"I like that."

"Good. It's decided, then," she says, and sips her coffee. The heater is on high and our cheeks are pink. The road is clear ahead and we are making great time.

"So, you know you're going to have to pee in the bushes," I say, not really looking forward to it myself.

"I'm an L.A. girl. I've done my share of barhopping, and believe me, squatting behind a parked car is many times better than those bathrooms."

"Quite the tough talker."

"California girls are tough too. Our wilderness is just different from yours."

"I don't doubt it."

We get to the ferry crossing and climb out of the Jeep.

Katherine puts on her waders and boots, and she's gotten just what I told her to. I can tell she tried them on before she came out. The suspenders are already adjusted, and with her hat and gloves on she looks like a natural.

"We're crossing the river and hiking upstream, looking for sockeyes today. Just catch and release. The salmon are spawned out now, but if you hook one, it'll put up a fight. Just remember to keep your tip up."

"Yes, ma'am," she says with a salute, her fly rod standing straight up next to her.

We wait for the ferry, which is just a platform tied to a rope. It has no engine; the current pushes it across the river. When we reach the middle of the river, I look downstream and the water is an opaque pale blue: glacier runoff the color of his eyes.

We reach the other side, and as we climb up the bank and look down, about three feet from the shallow water, the sockeyes are lined up like stepping stones.

I point at them with my pole. "They look easy to catch, but they're tired and heavily fished. They aren't biting. It's tougher than it looks."

But Katherine doesn't hear. Her mouth is open and she's smiling.

"There's so many." Her eyes are wide.

"The salmon wait for you to float your hook by and catch them right in the mouth. There are a few rainbows under the salmon, waiting for the hens to drop the last of their eggs. Drift the pattern beneath the salmon, and a trout might hit."

We start walking and we pick raspberries and round red berries that look like cough drops.

"Watermelon berries," I say, and drop some into her palm.

She puts them in her mouth. "They taste just like watermelon." She pulls a few more from the bush and we're off again, stopping every few paces to check the currents, and we reach Dottie's favorite spot on this side. There's a gravel bar that ends in a point beneath the water, and on either side the salmon rest, flicking their green tails against the current, their red bodies glowing beneath the water.

I hold aside branches so that Katherine can follow on the trail.

"Aren't the fish going to be wise to us if we're past all the other fishermen?" she asks.

"Depends on the fish. The king and silver salmon nest in the river, so you want to be downstream, where they aren't quite so wise. But the sockeyes nest in the sloughs and lakes upstream, so they need to pass us. The rainbows follow the reds, and so we follow the rainbows. And this way we're away from the crowd. Closer to nature."

She snags her line in a tree. We pull and get it loose.

"When a male salmon finds a female, he rubs against her and she drops her eggs, and he drops his sperm."

"Fish love. It's sweet," she says.

"But the rainbows are tricky. They follow the hens, and when the hens rest, the rainbows bump them to get them to drop eggs," I say, and leave my backpack in the grass. Gulls squawk and settle a few yards away from us. Dead fish float in the shallows. Their life cycle is over. They've mated and now they're done.

"Evil trout," Katherine says.

"When you fish trout, they're actually looking at your

fly pattern and hitting it, trying to eat it. When you're fishing salmon in the river, they're here to spawn and that's it. They aren't eating. What you're doing is dragging your fly across the bottom, across their sight line, hoping they open their mouths to breathe as your hook passes by their mouths."

"That doesn't seem fair," she says, and looks again at the fish, moving together as one long line upstream, against the current.

"Welcome to fishing," I say.

We wade out, our legs creating a wake. As we get deeper, the rushing of the river fills my ears. Katherine picks each step carefully, and I realize that I am simply walking. So many seasons I spent moving in the river like she is now. But now that I'm the expert, I move like Dottie does and like Steven used to—like I'm walking on land instead of fighting the water at each step.

I show her how to cast—a simple drift, letting the line go straight at the end of the arc, downriver for a few beats.

"This is a good time to fish because you can see them. Be aggressive. Picture where your weight and hook are and aim it at them." It is advice Steven gave me in Chinitna Bay as I stood there absently casting, going through the motions that I had done since I was a girl. Until that moment I thought Dottie was luckier than I was and that explained her hooking a fish at every cast. I figured Steven had what she had. I knew that the salmon weren't eating, and I thought it was all dumb luck. But when he told me, "Be aggressive. Go after them," soon I was actually catching fish instead of just fishing.

Katherine snags and struggles with the line.

"Pull hard and close your eyes," I holler at her. Her line comes up with a pop. It flings back toward her face and tangles at the end of her rod.

"Try again," I say. "And pull a bit faster; you won't snag as much."

She casts again and hollers, "I have one." Her bobber is underwater, but the line isn't moving.

"Reel!" I call out, and she reels, and at the end her hook has caught a stick tangled in someone else's fishing line.

"Stick fish," I say.

She mutters something that I'm sure wasn't intended for delicate ears like mine. I wait to start casting until she's able to cast out and let the line drift, then cast again without getting snagged much.

I walk away from her, upstream and just a bit deeper, the water lapping at my hips. I begin to cast too, and immediately I relax into the motion of it. I throw out and drift and for a few moments, I'm not aggressive. I am the little girl I was when I first began fishing this river. I catch myself daydreaming about a time when Dottie was about Gwen's age and Mom had us out here. Dottie yelled, "Moose! Moose!"

I looked up and about a hundred yards downstream a moose crossed the river. The river was rushing. It was deep that year from the endless snow of the winter, and I was sure the moose would drown. We all watched, giving up on the salmon for the moment, and that moose walked right through the water, though at the middle the water came to its chin.

It came out on the other side and Dottie cheered.

"Yay, moose!" she yelled.

"Yay, moose!" Mom called.

"Yay, moose!" I repeated.

But Dottie turned upstream and caught me with my line out, not casting or stripping the line in.

"Marty, you're scaring the fish. Cast!" she yelled.

"Oh my god, Martha, help!" Katherine yells, and I startle. My line is out like it was that day, making them wise to our flies.

"Martha, seriously, I have one!" Katherine's line is zigzagging into the middle of the river.

"Palm the reel. If it wants to run, let it. But don't give it any slack."

Katherine nods and puts her palm on the bottom of her reel. The fish is going, then pauses.

"Reel," I call, and begin bringing my line in. She reels madly, but the fish runs. "Palm," I call, and start moving toward her.

"Tip up!" I yell as she begins to point the rod at the fish. She'll lose him unless her rod is up straight and leaned slightly toward shore. They fight, and Katherine is gentle with the fish. She doesn't horse him like Gwen would, and she doesn't let him have too much line like I used to. She's like Dottie—a gentle touch.

"Now you need to back up toward shore. Keep him downstream from you, and back up slowly."

"I'm going to fall on my ass," she says, her eyes wide, staring at her tight line swirling with the water.

"I got you," I say, and stand behind her. I put my hands on her hips like my dad used to do with me when I caught a fish.

"Stepping back now," I say, and we both step back. "Reel," I say.

We move together back toward the shore, and after one last run, the fish is tired and Katherine gets it into the shallows. It's a large female, a hen. Her face is a deep green and her body crimson.

"She's a beauty," I say.

"I caught that," says Katherine, her eyes still wide. "Thank you for letting me catch you, Mrs. Fish."

"I think that was the ancient Inuit prayer when they caught a fish," I say, pulling the hook out of its mouth.

"Can I touch her?"

"Wet your hands first. We don't want her slime coming off."

Katherine wets her hands and picks the fish up. She puts it back in the water and watches as the fish wiggles once and swims away.

"I can't believe I did that." She smiles.

"You're a natural."

"Thanks." She practically runs back into the river. No more of the mincing girl steps.

We each catch a couple, and some bite but never hook up. We hike as we fish, trying slow-moving waters and different fly patterns. And while we're eating lunch, Katherine points to the sky as a single bald eagle flies over the river with a hunk of bright orange salmon in its mouth. Finally we're both tired, and we take the ferry across the river, back to the car.

On the drive home I put on the oldies station and we both know the words to most of the songs, but they're the easy ones. "I Heard It Through the Grapevine." "Respect."

"Yesterday," which I know because before he left, my dad used to play it each night before he went to bed. When Katherine knows the intro to Tina Turner's version of "Proud Mary," I'm truly impressed.

I pull into her driveway and she gathers her gear. I help her load the stuff onto her porch.

"Thank you," she says.

"You're welcome. Anytime."

"Seriously, you're a good friend to me. Thank you."

"You're a good friend to me, so thank you."

She smiles. "See you in a couple of days. And do your homework, or something." She waves to me and closes the door behind her.

I wave back and drive home, humming along with Bruce Springsteen. *"Tramps like us, baby we were born to run."*

# winter

Mr. Martin waits for the class to clear out.

"Martha," he says.

I'm in for it. I've been watching the trees grow brown daily. The bark beetle is taking them one by one, and I swear as I sit there I can see the trees turning. Sometimes he calls on me, and I can usually play the question back in my head and form an answer. I'm still doing homework, after all.

"Marty," he says, and leans against his desk.

"Mr. Martin." I notice for the first time his shirt is bright orange, still long-sleeved and no Hawaiian print yet, but the color is there. Like a salmon, he changes colors as the seasons move.

"I appreciate all of your homework, and you're doing well in class, when you pay attention."

"Thanks," I say, and glance once out the window. The third tree back from the woods' edge is a dark, dull green, and I know tomorrow it will be just a shade darker. I wonder if it will change by the end of the school day.

"What are you doing after school?"

I pull my attention back. "Going to work."

"I'm sure you are. I meant, after graduation, what are you doing? Steven mentioned last year he thought you would go for a biology degree, maybe marine biology."

"I never said that." I hadn't said it. It was something Steven had said I should do. He told me about his aunt who spent months on a boat tracking whales, trying to figure out where they go when they leave Alaska.

"That sounds like you," Steven said one night as I was shutting down the theater. The lights were off and he held a lighter to his face.

"I see a big gray mammal in your future," he said.

"I don't," I said, and blew out his lighter before I kissed his lips. A quick kiss before he could grab me and make me forget all the things I had to do before locking up.

"Come on, Martha, it's you. You're a scientist. Look what you did with the whale."

"I'm a girl who found a whale. Not even an endangered one. I didn't help with the oil spill. I don't spend my summers volunteering with the Department of Fish and Game. I'm just this girl," I said, and lifted his arm and tried to pull him out of his chair.

"Then what will you do? What will you do when

you're done with this crap? Sweeping floors and serving popcorn."

"Maybe I'll marry you and make babies and we can live in the bush and teach our kids from the old schoolbooks they send people on the bush planes." He went limp in the chair, so I took his feet and began to pull.

"That's not you either. You can't follow me."

He wasn't budging, and I wanted to get out of there. I wanted to change and pull my hair back and read a book.

"You tell me what I should do, and I'll do it."

"Be a marine biologist."

"Okay. Perfect."

"Stop it. I'll get up so we can leave, but you need to start thinking about this. Next year you start applying. You can't wind up like everyone else here. You need to leave. Get some real education."

"Okay," I said. And so Steven began calling schools for information on their biology programs. He brought me applications and brochures from schools all over. He handed them to me like Sean hands Dottie flowers, and I took them like I'd seen her take them. I'd kiss him and thank him and act like they were everything a girl could ask for.

"I have a year before I even need to apply," I said as he opened the applications and hunched over them with a black pen.

"Maybe I'm applying for me."

I leaned over him and saw that his name really was on the top of the form.

"You just said you didn't want to go to school."

"Martha, try to follow. We have similar grades. I worked on the whale too. I'll apply now, and if I get in to any of them, then you should apply to the same schools next year and you know you'll get in."

"This is ridiculous."

He looked up at me and placed his pen on the table. "Martha, I'll be gone by the time you need to apply to school. This is my way of guaranteeing a future for you."

"Do that on your own time," I said, and bit at the soft parts of his ears, his neck. He pretended to ignore me and then he couldn't and he seemed to forget about the applications, but later that afternoon I watched him gather them together as he left our house.

"Well, if you need a recommendation letter or any ideas about where to apply, I'd like to help," Mr. Martin says now.

"Thank you, but even if I did go to school, I'd have to have a scholarship." It seems like a logical thing to say, though I don't need a scholarship. Each year, as residents of Alaska, we receive a payment with our dividends from that year's sale of oil. Mom has saved each of our payments in separate accounts for us to do with what we wish when we turn eighteen. Dottie plans to use hers to move from Alaska. I picture her in California, sunglasses on, her toes in the sand.

As for Gwen, I believe she'll fall in love with the first boy she meets, sell all her things and travel the world with him.

For me, the money is just a number on a monthly statement. I can't touch it. I have no plans for it. It's not even completely real to me.

"University of Alaska has great scholarships," Mr. Martin says.

"I'll bet," I say.

"Have you gotten any material from them? I can help fill out any scholarship requests."

"I'll keep my eyes peeled," I say, just like I said to Steven in the past.

"You're not going to do any of this, are you?" Mr. Martin crosses his arms and shakes his head, then looks out to my trees.

"Beetles are taking more down," he says. "Think they should cut them?" I'm relieved. I don't want to disappoint him, but there is no way to explain about beauty and trees and comfort. I can't leave this.

I look out the window too. "No, the strongest ones will survive. And the youngest trees are okay for now. The cottonwoods will replace them."

He nods and sighs. "There's nothing I can say to you. I want you to do great things."

I start to collect my books. He can't understand that Alaska is great enough for me. It is greater than I could ever do, and I don't want to leave it.

I shove my things in my bag and nearly knock my desk over getting out of that classroom. The halls are filled and people look at me. There is quiet behind their eyes; they are simply watching what I will do next. And I can't let them see the anger I feel. They have no way of knowing who it is toward, but they'll guess my anger is for him, and then they'll think the worst. They'll forget that I loved him deeply, and I'm just this girl who was with him the day he died on a deserted beach miles across a freezing bay. I'm the one who couldn't help him.

I wait in the bathroom until the bell rings and the halls

are silent, and then I go out to the Jeep and drive away. I drive to the theater, and though Katherine's car is in the lot, I stop anyway. I go in and find her in the office with papers spread in front of her and a brand-new computer on the desk.

"My employee," she says, looking over the screen. "Why aren't you in school?"

"Half day," I say, and sit across from her.

"Yeah, right. Are you hiding out? Did the dog eat your homework or do you really need to be here?"

"I really need to be here."

She pauses. She rubs her head. "Why do you need to be here and not in school, and why should I let you stay here when you're truant?"

"I'm just having a bad day there. Teachers, students, all of them."

"That's not really telling me what I asked. I'll let you stay, no problem. But I want to know why."

"Let's watch a movie."

"I swear I'll call your school."

"You pick. I'll make popcorn."

"Look, Martha. You're going to have to tell me the truth eventually. Either that or I'll find it out." She stares at me right in the eyes and I would look away, but I'm locked in.

"I'll go," I say.

"I don't want you to go, but I told you the deal. Take it or leave it."

"I'm leaving it." And I walk away, back to my car. I drive out, and I want to kick up the dirt and pebbles of the parking lot and squeal my tires on the road, but as I turn, I see her at the door. One hand raised, palm flat and open to me. Not a wave, but asking me to stop, and I just can't quite.

And because it is truly impossible to run from anything and everything, when I get home I find a single envelope sitting on the kitchen table addressed to me from the University of Washington. I open it and inside there is a brochure for the school and a special letter from the marine biology department addressing me by name.

It begins by thanking me for my interest in their program, and just when I think it is a form letter, I read: *We received your letter describing the whale skeleton retrieval you coordinated* and I can't read anymore. I tear it straight down the middle and again and again until the pieces are too small. I gather them in my hands and I climb through the dying fireweed, the papers falling around my feet and my hair tangling in the dry branches. Cotton from the expired flowers floats around me and a single pheasant flushes from the brush. When I am at his steps, I drop more scraps. There are only a few left between my palms. I kick the door. I kick it again and the vibrations rattle up my shin. I kick it one more time, listening to the thud ricochet through the house.

And no matter how many times I kick it, it doesn't fall in, and more paper flutters from my fingers, and I kick one last time. My calves ache and my toes are numb and I let the final scrap fall. The door is covered now in black scuffs from my shoes and I kick it one last time because before this moment the door had been a perfect white Steven's mom had painted it the day she moved. Before that it was covered with blooms of splattered paint from a day long ago. Christmas. After his brother got a pair of pellet paint guns and during the dying light of the winter day, Steven and Tommy went out and shot each other and the snow and finally the door, exhausting their rounds of green, blue and red paint, so the door looked like a painting Steven and I had just studied in art history.

A few days later I go to work and find drop cloths on the floor of the lobby and Katherine standing on a ladder with a paint roller in her hand. The walls are a yellow just pale enough to be called butter, but a bit brighter so that not as many lights need to be on.

"Grab a roller," she says. "I have an old pair of jeans and a shirt in my office if you want them."

"I'm okay in this," I say.

The lobby is mostly done, so I work from the opposite end of the wall.

"You've been doing this all day?"

"Since this morning. Early. I got a wild hair up my butt."

"You should have called me."

"You had class, and I don't think painting the theater is worthy of your ditching."

"I like the color," I say.

"Nice, huh? I thought it would be good for the winter. Remind us of sunlight."

"We'll need it."

We paint. The only sound is the sucking of the rollers against the walls.

"How long have you been at this? You've done the ceiling and the bathrooms."

"I said morning."

"It just seems like a lot of work."

"Couldn't sleep."

"I understand." But it was bothering me, how much painting had already been done. Katherine's eyes had heavy bags. "Something you want to talk about?"

"It's this weird thing. I had a nightmare that I had woken up and my house was buried in snow. I knew I'd die in there." She dips her roller in the thick yellow paint.

"I have one like that, but in mine I'm drowning in the ocean."

She nods and slathers paint on her wall. "I think it's just scary to live here. I sometimes have the feeling that if I were to walk outside and into the fireweed, I'd be lost forever."

"Not around here."

"Maybe. But there are bears. Moose. I had this idea of blueberry picking and long walks following trails. But I'm too scared that I'll die out there."

I put my roller down; she's paused in the middle of a stroke. There's not much to say. She's right in some ways. There are bears out there. And moose. If you get too close to a cow and her baby, she'll charge.

"You could. But I guess you take your chances. You could have died on the freeway in California."

She lowers her roller and faces me. "But in California I thought I was in control. Up here, I know no one is in control. I just take my chances. I could die every time I step out of my house. Wild."

"Yeah. That's Alaska." I turn back to my wall and we

continue to paint long streaks of sunshine over the cloudy white. We paint as the sun goes down, throwing a rich orange glow into the theater.

And when people begin to gather, we collect our drop cloths and go to the bathroom and wash our rollers in the sink, our elbows touching and yellow milk water pouring through our fingers.

She opens the theater doors, then sits behind the ticket counter to take money and count change.

"The walls look great," says a woman from the post office. "Good for winter."

Katherine nods and smiles, but there's a sadness in her this afternoon. I recognize it. She misses someone. Maybe in her old life. Someone I'll never know.

Between customers she rubs her eyes with the back of her hand and stares out at the bay. And there are things I understand without needing to know. There are times in this life when the person you miss most is the person you used to be.

When the line trickles off, I pour her a Coke with some vanilla syrup. We walk out of the theater into the dying light and watch the final moment of sun as it passes below the horizon.

"Do you want to talk?" I lean in to her. She shakes her head.

"The walls are seriously beautiful."

"I'm just crazy," she says, and I put my arm around her and hold her tight, so tight that I know it hurts. Just like my mom did through the summer. Tight enough so she will remember that she is still here on earth and that there is someone who will hold her tight.

"Let's go in. I'm sure someone forgot to get a snack."
She smiles. "So beautiful here."

"Scary too."

"Yeah," she says. We wander into the lobby, and though it is dark outside, with the lights on it does look like sunlight in here.

"We did good today."

"Well," I say.

"Okay, college girl," she says, and pinches my arm. I open my mouth to say no, I'm not that girl, but she is still smiling a simply happy smile and I can't tell her otherwise.

"Friday night, after the last show, let's go out. A friend of mine plays guitar at the coffee place. Kind of folky stuff, but she has a good voice," I say.

"Oh, Martha, thanks, but I don't think so."

"It's not just a bunch of kids. There are people your age too. Everyone who doesn't want to drink at the Salty Dog."

"Well, what fun are they if they don't shower at the Laundromat and get blitzed at the dive bars on the spit?"

"We can have free coffee. Just as long as we let my friend into a movie."

"Who's getting the better deal there?"

"We'll get dessert too, okay?"

"Okay," she says. "We'll get out of here for once."

Friday comes and dark clouds gather. The temperature has dropped. Sleet. We run the afternoon movie—a cartoon about a space alien that looks strangely like a cat—and sweep the floors and lock the doors and begin the walk to the café. Sure enough, during the movie, a hard rain fell, then froze on the ground. Outside, my breath catches as I inhale.

"Cold," I say.

Katherine walks closer to me. "So, this friend of yours, how come she's never come in?"

"She wants to treat to coffee in exchange for a movie."

"We'll see if she's worth it," Katherine says with a wink. I've noticed her letting others in for free: a woman who waxes eyebrows and a man who lives in a shanty on the spit and a Russian girl with three kids pulling at her skirt. I've seen Katherine reject money. And if they insist, she hands their change back to them, folding it before they notice she hasn't charged them at all.

The café holds the only bright lights of the block. Trucks line the muddy parking lot, and through the café windows I see familiar faces from school and my friend Jen with her back to us and her elbow moving up and down in time. Steven said she was like a metronome. "Perfect time," he'd said. "I can set my watch to her."

"I swear if she closes her eyes and does a Joni Mitchell cover, I'm gone," Katherine says, pulling me toward the door.

"No, no Joni Mitchell. The young people don't like her."

"Good for you," Katherine says, and opens the door for me. The moist heat and Jen's voice swallow me, and both make my fingers tingle, the blood coursing hot from my heart to the farthest reaches of my veins.

We push through the people crowded near Jen. I'd like to say she sits on a stage, but she plays where they normally have tables, and there is a small semicircle of space between her and the crowd.

A couple moves together and we crowd in near them. As Jen sings she smiles at the crowd, picking people out—a boy who cleaned the whale bones but never returned after that stage was over. She smiles at a girl I recognize from the movie theater—she brings her small brother to the daytime kids' shows on the weekends.

And this time, instead of singing about love, Jen sings a silly song about sniffing roses that smell like noses, her head and arms bouncing along. She finds me in the crowd and crosses her eyes. Katherine laughs and Jen keeps bouncing. It isn't until I hear the chorus dedicating all of this to a boy that I am relieved that she still sings about love.

The song ends and Jen announces a break. She leans her guitar against a wall and waves to me. The crowd breaks up and she hugs me.

"Thanks for coming."

"We're so glad to be here. I brought the boss, so she could fine-tune the coffee-for-a-movie trade," I say, and introduce Katherine and Jen.

Jen shakes her hand. "Drinks are on the house. Anything you want."

"Well, Martha, you're a great date," she says to me, and to Jen, "I'll take a hot chocolate. And feel free to come to the theater anytime. You were great up there. We should have a musical interlude between the ads and the movie." Katherine raises her eyebrows at me. "Cool, huh?"

"Very," I say.

"Whenever you want, as long as I get in for free."

We head to the bar, and as I'm turned toward Jen I notice a man approach Katherine.

"I love that you're here." Jen hands me a mug. I nod, trying to hear what the man is saying to Katherine. But all I hear is a quick laugh from her.

Jen has another mug in her hand and she taps Katherine on the shoulder. Katherine turns and I see the man is her age. Blond hair and green eyes, and if he had a tan, I'd say it was a man she met in California. There is something familiar about him. He seems too young to be talking to Katherine, and then I remember that she's very young too.

"I'm glad to be here," I say. "Cool to see you up there." But I think, Who is the man talking to Katherine?

She thanks Jen and sips from the mug. "This is Ben. He just came up to me right now and decided to start talking," she says with a laugh. "This is Martha, she runs the movie theater. And this is Jen, she's the star of tonight's show."

"I've enjoyed your music," he says to Jen. And to me, "I've enjoyed your movies."

Jen smiles. "Good to meet you. Gotta go, don't know what I'm playing next." She moves away from us, tapping people's backs, smiling and hugging.

"I love your popcorn," Ben says to us both.

"Is that really appropriate to say to a couple of girls you just met?" Katherine says. And I laugh because the guy laughs, and because I don't know what else to do. I've never seen Katherine flirt before.

"I really do. Every time I pass through Homer, I stop in for a movie and the popcorn."

"Why are you just passing through?"

"Boring stuff. I live in Soldotna, but I work for the Department of Fish and Game, so I come through during the moose hunt and the start of salmon season to make sure all is well. Licenses are issued, the normal stuff."

"None of that's going on. What brings you here now?"

"I have a gun safety class I teach once a season. It happens to be this weekend."

And then I remember. He was one of the men who passed through briefly after Steven's death. The man who took the gun from me after we landed at the hospital. I was following Steven, forgetting what I held in my hands: our canteen, a single glove and the gun. Why had I taken that?

This man took it from me when I laid it on the floor in the waiting room.

"I'll mark it with your name," he said, and left. And because it wasn't mine, Steven's mom gathered it with the rest of his things as they were packing to leave Homer.

Jen says hello over the mike, and Katherine laughs once more after Ben leans over to her and says something only she's meant to hear.

"I'm not feeling well," I say into Katherine's ear.

"Is it your stomach?" she asks, suddenly turning all the way toward me, leaving Ben standing alone.

"Too much heat. And I have work to do tomorrow."

"We just got here. We need to see your friend."

"I want you to stay for us both. I really need to leave. I get vertigo," I say, remembering a movie in which the girl, a blonde with a perm, keeps saying that again and again.

"I need to walk you to the car."

"I'll be fine when I'm outside. Seriously. I just need to walk alone."

Katherine presses her lips together. She studies me and finally she says okay and hugs me. I press out of the crowd a bit embarrassed, but Jen doesn't notice. I move fast, away from that man. Outside I run, hoping he hasn't seen me, and as I drive home I try to figure out how much adults talk about their jobs. And hope there have been other cases since mine where that man would have to be. Bloodier situations. Anything that would make a better story than mine.

She doesn't mention him the next day and so I don't either, though as I look close at her when she thinks I'm focused on something else, she wears a smile.

"Jen's really awesome," I say while wiping down the counter.

"She was quite good. She looked for you after, but I told her you were sick and that you said goodbye."

"Thank you."

"No problem," she says with a raised eyebrow.

I turn to clean the soda machine, and as I wipe the towel over the already clean surface, I feel her looking at me now, like I had looked at her. Carefully watching. And so I rub hard, trying to get the chrome exactly perfect, but lint and string begin to stick.

"Was he nice?" I ask, my back to her and my arm aching as I try to dry the small drops of water before they become streaks.

"He was okay. Cute, but I think he's the type who doesn't read much."

"You think, or he said the last book he read was *Moby Dick* for junior year English?"

"He didn't say anything, and I suppose I could be making things up, but I'll say anything to make him seem bad."

"That's not fair."

"I'm a bad person," she says. "Are you trying to rub the plating off my soda machine?"

I put down the towel and turn to her and smile. "Sorry."

"It's nothing. I'll take the damages out of your pay." She comes to me and takes the towel, folding it over the sink. "Your friend mentioned to me that she was happy to see you out."

Now I want the towel back again, but Katherine is leaning against the sink, blocking my way.

"We lost touch over the summer." I try to brush past her, but she won't let me by.

"She said you seem happier than the last time she saw you. She thanked me for bringing you."

"That was nice of her."

Katherine pauses. She picks up the towel with a sigh, wets it and hands it back to me. "She said she misses you." She leaves me behind the counter with the wet towel in my hand. I hear her move upstairs to the booth. The previews need to be cut and the film taped.

And so I am left in the theater alone. I miss Jen too. I miss Steven, and with Katherine upstairs, I miss her too. I miss my mom and my sisters, and most of all myself, but there are just some people we'll never get back.

It begins snowing as I drive home, and it snows or rains for a week and a half. My mom is home from work each day when we get back from school, and Dottie grows restless. Normally these are the afternoons when she and Sean spend the daylight playing board games with Gwen, and as the sun sets they make their way to Dottie's room and I sneak past listening for noises, but there are none. And one afternoon I walked by as Sean was heading for the bathroom and inside I saw my sister, her mouth open and her eyes squeezed shut the way she used to sleep when she was young. Her face crunched like she was fighting it. And so I believed all they were doing was sleeping.

But with Mom home, Sean and Dottie will kiss once, a quick peck before he climbs into his truck to leave, and she sits on the couch, crosses her arms and sulks about whatever comes to mind.

"It's too damn cold around here."

"In other parts of the world, they still have a funny little thing called sunlight in the winter."

"Does the sofa smell like puke to you? Have you puked on the sofa, Martha?"

Then she goes to her room and shuts the door and IMs back and forth to Sean. Why they don't just call, or why he doesn't just come by and hang out in the front room like he does in summer, is totally beyond me. But they have their traditions, the things they do to stay in love. And how can I question that?

The last day of snow, right as the sun is setting and I'm leaving for work, I see the sun through the clouds. It's bright orange and hot blue in the sky, and white rays of light are shining on the ocean. And for the first time since it started raining, I can see across the bay and into Chinitna. The door opens and Gwen runs out with a pair of my socks on her hands and her hair in knots and ponytails all over her head.

"Look, Martha." She points with a socked hand across the bay where I look all the time. "You can see where Steven lives." She drops her hand and turns to me and smiles. "Dottie did my hair."

I don't know what to say. "I gotta go to work."

I get into the Jeep. I turn on the engine and put it in drive, and I pull away carefully, and slowly, and then more carefully.

When I arrive at work the smell of popcorn is already into the parking lot and the windows of the lobby glow yellow with daylight. A wind whips up and now that the cloud cover is gone, the air is even colder and my lips feel like they might just freeze off. I get to the door and notice the floors are freshly vacuumed, lines still in the carpet, and as I open the door Katherine jumps in front of me and points her fingers.

"Put 'em up, pardner," she says.

"Your money or your life," I say, drawing my own finger guns. I'm relieved. She wants to have fun just as badly as I need to. It is a special Friday night. Katherine has suspended the normal computer-generated, perfectly groomed movies we were showing for a grainy black-and-white western she found in the theater's storage.

Katherine buckles a toy holster around her waist and hands me a sheriff's badge.

"I don't think you have the right genre," she says, forgetting her guns and putting her hands on her hips.

"I'm the sheriff, I can say what I want."

"Well, I'm the bad guy, and I say you're a dork."

"Say what you want, but I'll have you arrested if you don't open up."

She pulls a face and opens the doors. Tonight, just as I expected, little boys with holsters and badges just like mine begin running through the door. Katherine takes the money and I serve the popcorn to the mothers and fathers. I listen as Katherine puts on her terrible western drawl to greet them, and then I hear her laugh.

I look up and she's talking to the man from the café. Ben wears a kerchief around his neck and a rodeo-size belt buckle.

"I told you I come here when I'm in town," he says, and Katherine smiles at him. She tucks her hair behind her ears and takes money from an older couple behind him.

"Grab some popcorn," she says, and catches my eye. She opens her eyes wide and smiles quick so he won't see.

"Hey, Martha," a woman from my mom's job says. "Can we have extra butter?"

"Yes," I say. But he hasn't taken his eyes off Katherine. When I'm done ringing the woman up, he is in front of me.

"Hey, I remember you, the night I met Katherine."

"Hey, yeah." I force a smile.

"I've been craving the popcorn ever since."

"Double butter?"

"Love it."

While I scoop his popcorn into the bag, I watch him, making sure he isn't watching me, but of course, he's watching Katherine.

I wave away his money and by the time he is done

grabbing napkins and salting his popcorn, Katherine has finished the line. He goes to her.

"Take him upstairs and show him how the movies really make it to the big screen," I say. She hesitates, but I nod.

"Hey, that would be very cool. A whole new movie experience," Ben says.

Katherine rubs her head. "Okay, but no touching any buttons or reels or anything."

"Not a problem."

And they go upstairs. I lock up the register and go into the theater. I take an empty seat in the back row so I can see people as they leave. The reels start and there is no preview, no credits, just a man and his horse, kicking dust up behind them, riding into town.

In the dark, listening to the soft clicking of the projector, my feet against the empty chair in front of me, I remember the way Steven smelled after a weekend of camping—a sharp iron smell like the fireweed after a moose has passed through.

He'd been gone a week, and as we hugged again he whispered in my ear, "There are two types of stories—man versus nature, and stranger comes to town."

I nuzzled his ear. "I'll take stranger comes to town."

He kissed me, tasting of coffee and fire. "I think mine is man versus nature."

I watch the dusty movie man get off his horse and tie him to a post. A woman drops a lace curtain in front of her face as soon as he looks up. She's been waiting for him, though he's not supposed to know. And as I watch his cracked, sunburned face turn from the window to the mountains he just rode through, I realize that Steven was wrong. There's only one type of story. Stranger comes to town. Man versus nature is just another name for it.


When the movie ends, I find Katherine and Ben sitting behind the snack counter, drinking soda and eating popcorn from the same bag.

"I hear there's this crazy wave around here. It just comes in like a freight train," Katherine says.

"Turnagain Arm," Ben says. "But it's not like California. There's quicksand underneath, and the tide really does come in with the speed and power of a freight train. Sounds like one too. You fall and you're dead."

What he doesn't say is the reason we Alaskans know of Turnagain Arm—not because of the wave itself, but because beneath that mucky sand there are millions of clams that no one can harvest. People try, and the thirty-foot tide comes in faster than they anticipate, and they are stuck in the sand. They are ripped apart at the legs. This is how tourists die in Alaska. These are the stories our parents tell us so we don't do foolish things like that.

"Hey, Martha, did you like the movie?"

"Pretty cool." I'm awkward standing there. I want to leave and I want to stay to make sure he doesn't tell her anything. But we all stare at each other and I realize that I do need to leave.

Stragglers file out of the theater and a man stops to shake Ben's hand.

"My kid just took your class. He said you were a cool teacher."

"I try," Ben says, and nods as the man leaves.

No one says goodbye to me. They have forgotten about me, and I am relieved, but then I realize that maybe they have forgotten about Steven too and for a moment I hate this place.

I get home and there's another letter from another college Steven sent away to for me and this one is even farther south. San Diego, California, as far south as I can go without leaving the country, and so I pull out the application. I write my name and address and start answering their questions, but just in pencil for now.



Mom's back at work doing office stuff, filing paperwork and writing bids for jobs for next summer, and so Dottie's been out again. Her cheeks are pink and her lips are peeling and cracked. She unravels herself from her scarf and hat and jacket and sweatshirt. It is black outside, though it is only five o'clock.

"You're home early," I say, looking up from my math homework. Calculus, I should say. Steven always made me say *physics* instead of *science class* last year.

"Cold out there. Snow maybe tonight."

"No clouds," I say.

"Snow tonight, I'm sure." She is down to her T-shirt and jeans, and she stands in front of the fire, hopping from one foot to the other.

"Seriously, why are you here?"

"Sean had some stuff to do at home. His dad needed a hand with the truck. Where's Gwen?"

"She found a friend. She's at his house. His mom is helping them bake cupcakes for his birthday tomorrow."

"A boyfriend?"

"Sounds like."

"We're a bunch of heartbreakers." Dottie swings her hips around and winks at me.

"Just you, Dottie Gelati."

"Listen, Martha, not to freak you out or anything, but I saw Sean's dad today and he was asking me about you. He was asking me about Steven."

I put down my pencil and rub my eyes. I want to believe that if I rub them hard enough, Dottie will disappear and come back in with a different thing to tell me. She will tell me that Sean proposed or that she finally got an A in a class and not what she is about to tell me and make my worst fears come true.

Sean's dad is with the Department of Fish and Game. He is a ranger and often goes for weeks at a time into the bush to count wildlife and to keep an eye on poachers. When we were kids he taught the free hunting safety class that Ben teaches now. Steven took Mr. Hale's class years ago and always said it was the smartest thing a hunter could do.

"Tell him I'm holding up well. Tell him I'm fine."

"He knows you're fine. He was telling me to tell you that there have been rumblings from his bosses that they need to investigate these things more. He wants you to know that they're taking a closer look at everything."

"What's there to look at? It was months ago. I talked to them when it happened."

"I know," she says.

Sean's dad came over to the house with a man from the police. They sat with me, and Mr. Hale put his arm around me as I cried. They asked me some questions, like if Steven was depressed before we left. How many years, to my knowledge, had he had guns. How long were we planning to stay in the bush. But mostly they sat and watched me cry and they talked to my mom about what a great kid Steven was and Mr. Hale said he would miss him. And then they left and I never heard anything else. All this time, I've been waiting, knowing that couldn't be all.

"What do they want? What did he say?"

"He said he doesn't know much, but that a hunter was shot last week in Seldovia, and another one died from exposure outside Fairbanks. They're worried that too many people are going out unprepared and uneducated. They aren't focusing on you."

"Steven was prepared. You know he was. He took Mr. Hale's class. He was fully licensed."

"All of the guys who have died recently were licensed."

"Listen, Dottie, the next time you're over there getting his son off, you tell Mr. Hale the truth. You tell him from me that Steven is dead, and that if he really is worried, maybe he should let his bosses know that he taught Steven all he knew, and that maybe they should be looking at their own men first." I crush my papers back into my book and slam it shut. My pencil flies at Dottie's feet and I turn to my bedroom, fear and shame burning in my throat.

She grabs my arm hard. She pinches my skin between her nails like Mom used to when we'd run into the snow without shoes.

"Martha, being mean to me and mean to Mr. Hale is not right, though I'm sure it feels good for the moment. Right now you need to think about this differently. This is a chance for everyone to see that Steven did everything right and that sometimes accidents just happen."

Her grip on my arm tightens, and I try not to make a noise, but she is hurting me.

"Dorothy, take your hand off me. And you have no idea about accidents."

She lets me go and I go to my bedroom and shut the door without slamming. It would give her too much satisfaction. I go into my desk and dig in my drawer beneath graded papers and pencils and pens and drawings Gwen has made me in school. At the very bottom sits the pile of applications. I find the one for California and finish filling it out, this time in pen. I fill them all out. I don't care anymore where they are—Chicago, fine, I'm used to the cold. Hawaii, great, I like the ocean. I check that I want early acceptance, ignoring the extra cash it requires.

I'm down to my last application when Mom comes home. The house is silent when she walks in. Gwen came home and went to bed long ago, and Dottie must have either snuck out or decided to catch up on some sleep.

I find Mom going through mail in the kitchen. She has her shoes off, but she's wearing panty hose and a skirt. I'm not used to seeing her dressed up for work, but when she's in the office, she wears a suit like she wears her jeans, comfortable and easy.

"Hey, Mom."

"Hey, Marty. I saw your light on. Lots of homework?"

"Not really. Just some reading."

"I'm glad to see you." She puts down the mail and pulls her fingers through my hair. "How are you doing?"

"Okay. It's time for me to apply to colleges."

"Ugh. Well, I don't want you to leave me. But I want you to go too. Get a real education. Use your big brain."

The house is quiet and we are whispering, though I don't know why. It's only seven-thirty, and if the lights were on, we'd be talking normally. But I keep whispering because I haven't been alone like this with Mom for months and I've missed it.

"I've applied to Anchorage. But other places too."

"I'll hope for Anchorage, but also someplace warm so I can visit you and tan these poor pale arms."

"It's a matter of being accepted."

She nods and washes her hands and gazes out the window. I look too. Our kitchen window faces Steven's house. His house is dark like I knew it would be, but I had hoped for a moment that the lights would be on to reassure me he was warm and safe.

"Mom, I need your help."

"Sure, what is it?" She dries her hands on a dish towel.

"It's about Steven. Mr. Hale told Dottie that the Department of Fish and Game wants to investigate his death more. Other hunters are dying, and they need to know why so many this year."

She closes her eyes and pinches her nose, then rubs her eyebrows.

"Bob Hale told Dottie this?" she says when she opens her eyes. I nod.

"I'll call him and find out what's going on. Don't worry," she says. "I'll take care of it." She kisses me on the head and rubs my eyebrows like she has just done to hers. She presses hard and the muscles in my forehead relax and my shoulders drop.

"Finish applying to schools. Give me a list of where the checks need to be written and how much. Apply to them all. Pretend money is no object."

"Okay, Mom. Thanks."

She leaves the kitchen and I sit watching Steven's house and the sky beyond, and if I sit really still I can see the pink and orange smear in the sky. The northern lights. And so I go outside and into the cold and dark over to his deck and I watch those lights in the sky shimmer to purple and green and then back to black, when they disappear.

When I get back, Mom's in her room on the phone, mumbling "Mm-hmm" and "Okay."

"Bob," I hear her say, "there's nothing to investigate. It was a tragedy, but there is nothing more to know."

She is quiet, listening. And then she says, "Bob, she's just a girl. She has her future. She's applying to school. She grew up with your kids. It could have happened to Sean. Remember that time he nearly took your toe off during target practice that summer?" She listens again.

"Please help us. Help Marty and Dottie and Gwen. Help us all."

There is silence and she whispers thank you and hangs up. She sighs and then goes into the bathroom, and so I go to my bedroom and pull all the covers over my head and though I'm sweating, I close my eyes to sleep, hoping that in the night I will simply disappear.

But late, after the house is still, I wake out of a black dream, and for a moment I'm unsure why I'm awake. And then I feel her in my room.

"Dottie?" I whisper. She lies down, her head on my pillow.

"Hey," she says. Her breath is warm on my face, smelling a bit yeasty like a beer drunk long ago. I have to tell her.

"It was me," I say. She pulls the covers over her. Her jeans are rough on my bare legs. "I'm the reason he's gone. The gun was in my hands."

Now that it's out, I am light, like I was that afternoon after the gun went off, and before Steven sank to the ground. The seconds of anticipation, wondering what I'd hit.

She sighs and tucks some hair behind my ear. "I know," she says. "I've always known."

"How?"

"I'm your sister." She puts an arm around me and breathes deeply. I match her breathing and fall asleep at the same moment she does.


Dottie's back in her bed when I wake. On my way to the bathroom, I find Mom putting on her coat, ready to leave for work. She rubs some sleep from my eyes and tells me, "It's getting taken care of." She smells like roses, like spring and sunshine. I trust her.


During Mr. Martin's class I notice large holes in the woods where some trees have been cut and some have simply fallen, taking others down with them. But there are smaller trees, bright green, beneath them. Baby trees, and Mr. Martin was right. More will come and survive and eventually be immune to the bark beetle, but for now, through the open patches, I can watch the town of Homer go by. Picking up mail at the post office, buying milk at the market. Cars I recognize from the theater parking lot or dropping kids off at Gwen's school.

Class ends and I wait for everyone to go. Mr. Martin's wearing a Hawaiian print shirt, but not as bright as the ones he'll wear next month. This one has a black background with wide-open burgundy flowers. He wears a long-sleeved shirt underneath.

"All right, Miss Martha. What is it now?"

"I'm doing what you said. I'm applying for schools and I need a great letter of recommendation. And I need it now."

"Did you get one from Mr. King? I'm sure he'll write a great letter."

"He's working on it, but I don't know how long it will take. I have a week to get everything together for early admittance."

"Well, this is a change."

"A girl can change her mind," I say, trying to sound funny and not like my whole life is riding on this.

"Where are you applying?"

"All over. Away from here."

"You'll be happier. I'll write you one tonight, have it for you tomorrow. But in order to get it, you have to answer three questions in class without my calling on you."

"Okay," I say. It's a small price to pay.

• • •

Sean and Dottie agree to pick up Gwen from school so I can get to work, though I argue with them, telling them I won't be late to work if I get her. But they both know my schedule. They know it is my day to open and that I would be very late if I got her.

Katherine's car is in the lot when I get there, and the door is unlocked.

The lobby is empty. "I'm here to steal the popcorn machine!" I yell.

"It's that good, isn't it?" Katherine yells back from the projection booth. "Hurry up here before Ben and I make a complete mess of this film."

I stop. He's here, in my theater.

"Martha, help!"

I head up there and find them with bits of film scattered around the floor.

"I'm trying to show Ben how to splice in the ads."

"I think it looks fine," he says.

"You can totally see that annoying white line when we project it. Let Martha do it. She's the master film splicer." She stands and offers me her stool and I sit.

I show Ben like Mr. Carter showed me. Breathe in once, hold, and exhale when you cut, and then splicing is the easy part. Ben is close to me, watching.

"We only have two ads on this reel," I say to distract myself. They've completely cut apart a soda short.

"We're fine, they'll never know. It isn't like Jimmie's floatplane ad or something."

Ben breathes in once and cuts one more ad into the strip. And I can tell that it is perfect.

"Ha!" he says, and pushes his stool back. He grabs

Katherine around her waist and stops short of kissing her, though I can tell it's for my sake and not hers.

The phone rings downstairs and I go for it, but Katherine runs in front of me.

"The plumber! I've been waiting on this call all day."

"What's wrong with the pipes?" I ask as Katherine runs to the phone.

"My house," she calls back. "Make sure that guy doesn't ruin everything."

"A pipe burst last night because she didn't insulate them before the winter," Ben says, rolling his eyes. "Damn Californians." He smiles and laughs.

"Listen, you don't know me from the whale. You know me from the summer. My boyfriend was shot in the bush. You were at the floatplane when we were dropped off."

His smile fades and I listen as Katherine keeps talking. The plumber is a regular and I can hear her teasing him about his prices.

"I know," Ben says. "But that's a tough thing for a kid to go through, so I thought I'd keep it to myself."

"They're looking into it again. Steven's death." I pick up a reel and press my thumbnail into the tight roll of film.

"I know. Bob Hale's taking care of it."

"My sister's going out with his son."

"His boy's a real good kid."

I nod, pressing deep. The film is sharp under my thumb.

"I'm taking care of it too," Ben says. "Katherine loves you a lot. She thinks you're great. Not to worry."

"Ugh!" Katherine calls from downstairs. She runs back

up. "Costing me a small fortune, but I guess I learned my lesson."

"Ben's a film-splicing genius," I say.

Katherine smiles at him, and then at me. "We're grabbing a bite before the show. Want to come? Pizza's on me."

"I know, I've seen you eat."

She crosses her eyes and smirks.

"No, I'm going to stay here. Sweep a bit."

"Oh, Martha, why don't you just do some homework on the clock. Don't sweep."

I take her arm and lead her to the door. Ben follows and jogs to the restroom.

"I've applied to a school in San Diego and I wanted to know if you've been there," I tell her as she puts on her coat.

"You've applied to schools? I'm so glad you did. That's really great. Congratulations." She smiles and I fix her collar.

"I'm applying to several, but I thought if you had good things to say about San Diego, I would consider it if they accepted me."

"Well, I moved from Southern California, so maybe I'm not a good judge."

"That's fair. I just think I need to get out of here. See the world."

"Why? Alaska is more about the world than San Diego."

"I'm not just thinking of there. Really all over."

"I thought you loved this place. You're a true Alaska girl, remember?"

"I think you called me that."

"Nothing wrong with it. Something I wish I could be, but let me tell you something as someone who has seen this world you're talking about. There is no place as beautiful as this. This place holds all the beauty of the world. Right here, girl. Believe me."

"I'll believe it when I see it." I try for a light tone, but she cuts me a sharp look.

"You have no idea. But let me know if I'm wrong."

Ben comes out of the restroom and grabs his coat.

"Go," I say, and she hugs me.

"I'll miss you."

"It's just dinner," I say, and she smiles. Ben holds the door for her.

I sweep until I hear gravel kick up in the lot. And then I put the broom away and wander up to the projection booth.

In a locker with old film splices and commercials I find a heavy metal canister. *Save* is written in big red letters that I recognize as Mrs. Carter's script. It's always been up here for me. And I rarely open it. I'm so afraid I'll tangle the film, or the light from the projector will burn a hole straight through. So I thread it carefully and once it begins I run down the stairs and into the theater.

It's a black-and-white French movie from the sixties. It's about a man who races cars and a woman who loves him very much. It's my mom's favorite movie, and when I started at the theater we showed it one night. I sat with Mom and Dottie, and Mom held both of our hands and cried from the beginning on the beach to the end with the man alone. At the end, she used our sleeves to wipe her tears.

"It was a good cry," she said. And now the same beginning plays on the screen and I slink down in my seat and I watch the man and the woman fall in love and I watch them separate and I am relieved that I'm not the only one.


Three days pass before Mr. Hale turns up at our house.

Dottie has ridden home with me because Sean is in an after-school study group. Gwen is singing the peanut butter and jelly song over and over in the backseat, and we sing along with her until we pull up to the house and Dottie and I see Mr. Hale's truck. Gwen keeps singing and Dottie takes my hand.

"He doesn't have the ranger truck. It's just him."

"Okay," I say.

*"Peanut butter—and jelly, jelly,"* sings Gwen.

"Mom's talked to him. Everything is okay," says Dottie.

*"Jelly, jelly,"* chants Gwen.

"I know."

"I'm with you. I won't leave you."

*"Peanut butter,"* Gwen calls at the top of her lungs.

"Let's go."

Dottie grabs Gwen. "Go draw me a picture. I want to see a fish's insides. Use a lot of red." Gwen is off like a shot through the house and into her room, and Dottie and I walk into the kitchen and find Mr. Hale drinking coffee with Mom.

He wears his normal clothes—jeans and a flannel shirt—and I see no notebook or tape recorder. He has no badge ready for me, and I exhale.

"Hi, girls," he says.

"Hi, Mr. Hale," Dottie says for us both.

"Do you want us to go?" asks Mom.

"No," I say, still holding on to Dottie.

"There's no reason for you to leave. I'm here unofficially. I'm just here to tell you what will happen in the coming weeks. No questions. Just here to give some advice and to prepare you."

"I thought you took care of things," said Mom.

"I took care of what I could. I refocused the inquiries on a hunter up in Sitka. I told them that Steven hadn't been hunting in years and was probably out of practice. I said I knew him and that I'd look into this case. But there are still steps. There is a process."

"We'll get her a lawyer. We'll do anything we can. Maybe Fish and Game should be looked into. Maybe they shouldn't be so lax as to let a seventeen-year-old boy into the bush with a bear gun," Mom says. Her fingers are white, clutching her coffee mug.

"Should we let people go out there totally unarmed?" Mr. Hale says back.

"No, Mr. Hale," Dottie says, dropping my hand. She sits next to him at the table. "We just want Martha to be protected. She did nothing wrong."

I nod once, hoping to look convincing, but there is so much I did wrong. Or more likely, so much I could have done that I didn't. No tourniquet can stop a gut wound. I could have pressed the towel into the wound harder, but I had no strength. Or I could have repositioned the gun higher or a hair to the left or the right. I could have told him that I didn't need practice instead of asking him to hold my arms steady because I wanted to hear his breath in my ear.

Or I could have been the one. I would happily go back and step a foot to the side and be where Steven was in that moment, that split second.

"I know people complain about the bureaucracy of government," Mr. Hale says, "but in this case it's a good thing. Basically it will take months for a decision to come down about bringing in the police. And we hope you'll be gone by then. Your mom says you're going away for school?"

"I am," I say. Dottie looks surprised. I haven't told her yet, afraid she'll be mad, or worse, jealous.

"Good," he says. "I'll interview you once, and then my supervisor will interview you and I'll be there. And after that, if he's not satisfied that it was an accident, they'll forward that info to specialists. And so on. But like I said, you'll be long gone, and what will they really do? Ask an eighteen-year-old girl to leave her school in the Lower Forty-eight to come to Alaska for a few questions? No."

Mom hasn't moved. Her fingers still grip the mug and I feel like I've been cemented to the kitchen floor, forced to live this one moment for the rest of my life. But I know this can't be true, there are so many other moments I am forced to live over and over. The moment I looked down and somehow Steven was in my lap, his eyes staring up at the wide blue sky above us, his blood warming my jeans. The moment I heard the crack of the gun and Steven grunt once and tell me "I'm okay," and I believed it, until I saw different. And the moment hours before, waking up with him next to me, breathing in my ear, promising me beauty for the rest of my life.

"This is yours, this is ours," he said of the patch of

beach we'd slept on. The fireweed bursting into purple and red. The conifers alive and bright green.

Dottie is the only one of us who moves. She nods and she asks questions like will I have to go to his office or will he come here. "Should Martha get a lawyer?" she asks.

"This is a casual visit. And as a friend, my interview is just between us. I'll tell you if that isn't a good answer."

Dottie nods again, and I nod too.

And Mom releases her coffee mug. "Okay, Bob. Thank you."

He touches her arm and says, "I guess I'll be going. I'll call a week ahead of time and schedule an interview. I'll put it off as long as I can."

He leaves us and we are all quiet. Dottie is up and making dinner. Gwen comes in with her drawing finished and ready for Dottie to put it up on the fridge. It is a careful drawing of a female salmon with bright orange eggs clustered in her abdomen and a small purple heart under the clear web of her ribs.

"It's perfect," I tell Gwen.

"Thanks, Martha," she breathes into my ear as she hugs me. She smells like wax from her crayons.

We eat, listening to Gwen tell us about school and all the boys she loves.

"What kinds of cars do they drive?" Dottie asks.

"Trucks and Jeeps," says Gwen. They compare eye color and hair color and the kinds of music they listen to and Gwen makes up bands and singers and songs. And when they are done and Dottie has cleared the dishes, Mom turns to me, her mouth a straight line and her eyes narrowed.

"I'm calling Dad," she says.

"Come on, Mom," I say.

"What's he going to do?" asks Dottie.

"I don't know, but we need some help. We need someone else on our side. I can't think of anyone who will do it with no questions."

Dottie shakes her head and turns back to the dishes, and there is nothing I can say. She's right, no one else will really take our side. There is no one else who will join us without questions.

She calls him the next day. He says he has vacation time coming, so he'll come to us when we need him. He'll put in a request for some desk duty too, so he can be free whenever Mr. Hale calls.

"I can come by floatplane if it's an emergency," he tells Mom. And we are all right. He never asks why we suddenly need him. But he is there, and I suppose because I've never needed him before, I had no idea that he's been there for us all along.


The shortest day of the year comes during winter break. The sun rises around ten-thirty, and this suits Dottie, who has been sneaking into the house late at night and waking with the sun. I, however, still wake at the same time I would if I were getting ready for school. It is night then, though around eight the sky begins to lighten, preparing for the sunrise. And for the shortest day of the year, Katherine is running a beach movie marathon.

"Have some fun in the sun," the marquee reads. We show Frankie and Annette, *Endless Summer, Point Break,*

*Aloha Summer* back to back. The theater is crowded because not only is the sun dim, but also thick, gray clouds are gathering. It looks like snow to me, though the people in line say no, it isn't cold enough. But when I step outside I cough because the air is sharp with cold.

Katherine and I watch all the surf and summer movies from the back row. During a surfing sequence I whisper, "Is this what life in the sun is all about?"

"Yes and no," she whispers back.

"Are there this many blondes?"

"Yes, but not naturally."

"Does it make you homesick?" I ask.

"God, no," she says. "Oh, this is the worst part." She covers her eyes and I look up to see the blond boy's board break in half from a wave and then the camera cuts to the boy under the water pushed down and into the coral reef. He's hurt, but he's swimming up, and because it is just a movie I think how warm that water looks. How turquoise, and the hot yellow sunlight filters deep, lighting red, purple and green fish. Katherine is wrong. There is beauty elsewhere. Just a different type.

And when I get home from our summer marathon, the sky opens and snow falls. Gwen runs out the front door and into the moonlight, white covering her hair and hands.

"Snow, Martha," she says.

"Snow, Martha," Dottie calls from behind Gwen, and runs barefoot into the driveway and dances with her. I lift my face to the falling snow. It is so cold. The flakes burn hot on my skin, and as I open my eyes I notice a light on at Steven's house.

There's a brown station wagon in the driveway. It's the

Realtor who often leaves cards on our front door with notes about tourists who fall in love with Alaska on their first visit and would we be willing to sell.

"What's she doing?" I ask Dottie.

"She's trying to sell their house," she says, and catches a single flake on her fingertip. "It'll be better for everyone if you can't sneak into that house anymore."

"I don't do that." Snow falls on my face and into Dottie's hair. I shiver, but steam rises from her head.

"Okay, whatever. But it's time you quit. There's nothing else to do."

"Snow angels," Gwen calls, and before I can stop her she falls backward and I expect a howl because the snow isn't close to deep, but Gwen has landed on a patch of thick grass and she is kicking her legs and flailing her arms. Dottie runs to her and flops down too and so I follow. I lie down slowly, not sure what is underneath me, but I too have a soft surface and so we all flop and wave. Snow falls onto my eyelashes, and my sisters squeal. The sky is black, so rich and thick it looks warm. It feels as if I can see for miles into that blackness, the stars glimmering white, and as my eyes adjust, there are millions of stars. Billions. And it is time to move on. I have no choice.

Because it is winter, the stores on Pioneer have strung Christmas lights across their windows, and this is supposed to be cheerful, but I can't see it. The roads have been plowed so much that large, dirty banks of snow line the road, and the sun manages only a dim light, barely a wink, in Alaska's direction. A few green and red lights will never make these days easier.

The travel agency advertises a round-trip to the Bahamas, hotel included, for $2,367.19. "Low, Low, Low," the sign reads. This is the exact amount our Alaska Permanent Fund checks will be when they come on the first of the year. The mechanic has a similar offer for an engine overhaul, and the floatplanes can fly a family of six all over the West Coast for the same amount.

And when the checks come, some people will blow it all in one shot. But many in this town will drink it away slowly. The parking lots of the bars will be full the whole winter, and the number of accidents due to "snow" will increase.

But when my check comes, it will go into my bank account, where the others have gone for the past seventeen years. They go to gather interest and wait for me until I am ready to use them. I thought I'd use them to buy my own cabin, but now I need that money.

For Christmas, Sean, Dottie and I go out to get a tree. Though there are tree lots in Alaska, we drive out like we always do and get our own. Sean brings snowshoes for us, and he drives us out on the Sterling Highway halfway to Cooper Landing and parks by the side of the road. The sun is just rising, a pale yellow in the gray sky, as we strap on our snowshoes.

"We could just find some beetle kill," I say, not looking forward to the hike in and the sap on my hands on the way out.

"It won't smell good. It won't smell like Christmas," Dottie says.

"But then we're not out killing random trees, and the ones we kill are the strong trees, they're the ones that will survive the beetles."

"Come on, Marty. Would you rather have a bright green tree or an ugly brown one?"

"Some aren't brown all the way."

"Martha, stop."

And I do, because she is right. The felled beetle trees are brown and spotted and look dead.

We march single file into the woods. We have an ax and a handsaw. It takes a moment to get used to the snowshoes again. I step once on the back of Dottie's.

"Flat tire," she yells. Her voice echoes off the snow, cracking the quiet, dim air.

But I remember to step wide and keep my hips underneath me instead of leaning forward. Soon I am sweating.

"*Hi-ho, hi-ho,*" Sean begins to sing, and Dottie pelts him with a snowball.

"Great, now that song will be in my head the whole day," she says, grabbing his arm as he walks.

Tree branches hang heavy with ice and snow, and Dottie stands beside the smaller trees. She and Sean decided that we're looking for a tree just a few inches taller than she is. We have to find it soon, because we'll have to drag it back through the snow, and we don't want to carry it too far.

We find one and Sean grabs the ax and begins to swing. It's a bright green, the needles holding all the sunlight from summer and fall. Dottie wanders off into the woods to pee and I sit and watch Sean hack away at the trunk. He swings the ax like my father did in the years he had time off during Christmas, and like I'm sure his own father did each year until Sean was old enough to handle it on his own. He holds the ax high and sweeps it down in one smooth arc, taking out a piece each time.

And when there is enough room, Dottie grabs the handsaw and begins pushing and pulling. This is her favorite part. When we were kids, Dad would let her stand between his arms and she would hold his wrists while he sawed.

Her sawing is the only sound, and I lie back and watch the sky. It isn't bright enough to hide the stars. As my eyes adjust, and the snow grows warm beneath my head, I can pick out whole constellations.

"Timber!" Dottie calls, and the tree cracks once, then falls with a hush.

"It's a good tree," Sean says, and kisses Dottie on the mouth.

We all grab the tree and hike back out, falling into step. We are quiet. The only sounds are our steps and ice falling in the forest.

On the way home, several cars are parked by the side of the road, with families buttoning up winter gear. It's a tradition, I guess. Another way to pass a cold, dark day.

Gwen puts herself in charge of the tree decorating. She directs all of us where to put bows and lights and balls. When we are done, the bottom half is heavy with ornaments, because for every one we hang, she hangs three.

"Perfect," Gwen says.

"Perfect," Dottie says.

"I think it's the best tree ever," says Gwen, folding her arms and nodding.

"That's what they all say." I grab her around her waist

and pull her onto my lap. Her arms are wiry and strong and she's hot like she has a fever. But she's fine. This is her little body, and I put my face in her neck and snuffle her like a dog, breathing in her fireplace smell. She giggles and squirms, but lets me hold her. My sister. My happiness.

Later that night, I am in bed and just asleep when Dottie reaches a cold hand under my blankets and grabs my ear.

"What the hell?"

"Shhh, get up." She is dressed, and in the moonlight I can see she wears glitter on her eyelids.

"Dottie, if you woke me to ask if your shoes match your skirt, I'll kill you right here."

"Get up, you mean girl. We're going out."

I lie back down and pull the blankets over my head.

"There's a party tonight. One of the guys on the football team has the house to himself."

"Give me a break. Let me sleep."

"I want you to be there. Sean wants you to be there. You can be a big lump for the rest of the winter, but tonight I'm the boss and you have to get up."

I lie for a second longer before I feel another cold hand grab my toes.

"Dottie, why tonight?"

"Why not?" she asks. Her breath is minty. "I'm a butterfly." She turns around and she has Gwen's wings from a Halloween costume a few years back strapped to her shoulders.

"You're a freak."

"C'mon," she says. She stands in the moonlight, shimmering, the wings floating over her shoulders.

"You can borrow my wings."

"You keep them. You're the butterfly."

I wear jeans and try for just a T-shirt and sweater, but Dottie can't be stopped and she hands me one of her torn, thrift-store shirts, hot pink with *Hollywood* ironed on in glitter.

She rubs black eyeliner over my eyelids and a deep red lipstick over my lips.

"You look perfect," she says. "Very California. Rock-and-roll."

"Thanks, Dot."

She hands me her tall boots. "Good thing we're both naturally beautiful or we would have missed the party. It would have taken us too long to get ready."

I kiss her cheek as she slowly opens the door.

"Watch the face," she whispers.

"Seriously, you're the best."

"I know."

She takes my hand and we creep down the stairs, and once we're in the drive we break into a full run down to the road, where Sean's truck sits, the lights off, waiting for us.

The cab is warm and Sean leans over and ruffles my hair.

"I knew you'd come, Martha."

"Just no making out in front of me. This is my sister."

"No prob," he says, kicking up gravel as he makes a U-turn and we head to town and wind onto the hill above school.

The house glows yellow on the hill, and trucks and

Jeeps are parked all over the road. It's an A-frame house that I recognize from an article in the *Homer News* about gardens. As we walk up, the garden now is covered in plastic held down by river rocks.

Dottie grabs Sean's hand and mine.

"Here we go," she whispers. My stomach drops. I want to turn around. Make an argument for leaving that would go something like, I see these people all school year, why would I want to see them on my break? But Dottie is pulling us in.

People are clumped together in groups, drinking beer from plastic cups, and bowls of food sit out on a table. Dottie kisses girls' cheeks as she makes her way through the crowd. Sean shakes hands with guys and smiles and nods at girls. They know everyone. I had no idea.

And people say hello to me too. They know my name, though I don't know theirs.

The Beatles play, and then an old Rolling Stones song comes on.

"I love this song," Dottie says. It's one Dad used to play for us. Him on air guitar, us dancing on the couch.

Dottie stands and grabs Sean and pushes the group he's talking to into the living room, where she dances in the center of them. Her wings bounce with her, and more people come over and dance. Maybe their dads played the same games with them.

The lights dim and the song changes and more people dance. They dance through all the songs Dad used to play, the songs I hear now on the oldies station and wonder why I know the words.

The room grows hot, humid with sweat and spilled

beer, and I move to the window. The bay is socked in with fog, and all I can see is the roof of the school and the lights in the parking lot shining on empty asphalt. I lean closer, looking into the windows of the school. From this angle, if the school were lit, I would just be able to see the whale hanging in midair. Its ribs, polished bright white, clean. My whale.

"Hey, Martha." A boy moves to the window, blocking my view.

"Hey," I say. I recognize him from the halls, but I don't know his name.

"Tim," he says.

"Hey, Tim." His light brown hair hangs in curls over his forehead. His brown eyes are sleepy-looking. I'm sure there's a quiet girl at this party who thinks of him as her Holden Caulfield, making up stories about how sensitive he is.

"I like the whale. I like seeing it every morning when I come in." He looks over to the school, at the angle I was just seeing.

"Thanks. But it was the whole science department."

"I wanted to tell you that you did a good job."

"Everyone did."

He touches my arm and smiles. "Say what you want, but I'm telling you that you did a good job." He raises his eyebrows and smiles. His teeth are a little crooked.

"Thanks," I say.

"Dance?" he asks. It's a slower song and couples are dancing close together.

"I don't think so."

"Do it for the whale."

I laugh despite myself. As the song plays I recognize it from a mix Steven made me before we left for Chinitna Bay. I stop laughing when I realize I just can't.

"No. Thank you."

"Maybe later," he says, and drops his fingers from my arm. He jams his hands into his pockets and walks away, and I hope that girl with the crush on him intercepts him just now. But he just blends into the dance floor.

And when the lights are low and the windows fogged from the sweat of our bodies, Dottie sits next to me on the couch.

"Having fun?" she asks. The glitter from her eyelids has drifted down her face and onto her neck and arms, so now all of her skin shimmers.

"I am," I say.

"I saw that guy talking to you."

"He was nice."

"Cute," she says.

"There's a girl waiting for him."

She nods and looks out at the party. People are draped over the couches, and couples still dance. Sean moves to us and sits on the coffee table.

"Ready to go?" Dottie asks.

"I am," I say. "Thank you for bringing me."

"No problem."

I hug her. I'm more grateful than I can say for one night out. One night warm. One night when I'm not alone.

We drive home and they drop me off at the front door.

"I'll be back later," Dottie says. "The door squeaks halfway. Put your hand over the jamb and it should be okay."

"I know."

The door does squeak, but I don't put my hand over the jamb. I walk into the dark house, but there is light glowing in the kitchen and I find Mom. She smiles when she sees me.

"You look great," she says, and laughs. A cup of coffee steams in her hands. "Were you sneaking in?"

"I was."

"You should know that Dottie is the worst at sneaking out, followed by her older sister. If you think I don't hear the both of you leaving in the night, you're crazy."

"We don't sneak out," I say, and I can't stop a smile.

"Oh, right. Did you have fun at the party? Was it at Janey Marshall's house? I know her son is on the football team and she's out of town for the week."

"Mother, I was at the library."

We both laugh. "Did you have fun?"

"A boy talked to me."

Mom raises her eyebrows, and I shake my head no. "He was very cute, but just not exactly right."

"It's okay." Her hand is warm on mine. "Dottie out still?"

"Yeah."

"Okay, get to bed."

I kiss her on the top of the head and leave her in the kitchen. How many nights has she waited up like that for Dottie? How many nights for me? I can't believe I never knew. But I suppose in the night, all houses have a life, and for mine, that life is my mom. Always waiting up for us.

•   •   •

And on Christmas Day, Gwen wakes us, though it is late for a Christmas morning, nearly eight.

Dottie rubs her eyes as Gwen pulls her to the living room, where Mom has left the tree lit from the night before.

We let Gwen unwrap one present—a game of Operation. Then Mom tells her to take a break.

"We need coffee," she says, and Gwen sits in the middle of the kitchen floor giving herself electric shocks with the toy tweezers while Mom makes Dottie and me coffee. Dottie's eye makeup is smudged across her cheeks, and her eyes are swollen.

Though I'm tired this morning, the coffee wakes me enough to endure some electric shocks with Gwen. Dottie rests her head on her knees while Mom makes breakfast. We sit down to eat and there's a knock at the door. We all pause. It's rare to have a visitor so early. Dottie looks up from her knees and at Mom, who stands, spatula in hand, waiting for another knock. And another one comes.

"I guess Santa has come a bit late this year," Dottie says, unfolding herself from the chair.

"I didn't hear reindeer," Mom says, and we all move into the living room while she opens the door.

And Dad is on the other side.

"Ho, ho, ho," he says, holding packages. "No one shoveled the roof, so Santa left these by the garage."

Mom accepts a kiss on the cheek, and Gwen grabs him at the knees. He shuffles in.

"Hey, Dad," Dottie says, hugging him over the packages.

"Martha," he says when he puts them down and grabs me around the shoulders.

"Dad, what brings you around?"

"Christmas cheer."

He sits with Gwen in his lap and begins handing out presents as if he had just stepped out for some firewood. Mom sighs and lets him pretend that he has. And Gwen tells him about the snow, about a gull she found in the middle of the road.

"Flat like a pancake," she says.

"Like a pancake? That flat?" says Dad.

Gwen gets the bulk of the presents, and Dottie gets gift certificates to the department stores in Anchorage. I get a journal from Dot and a set of barrettes from Gwen.

"She picked them out," Mom says.

"Perfect." I clip one into my hair, where it pinches my scalp.

I too get gift certificates from Mom, but when all the presents are unwrapped and Dottie has taken Gwen to get cleaned up and dressed, Dad hands me one last present. It's wrapped and I know it's another book. I open it and it is a notebook, old and frayed, the pages swollen from water damage. Inside, my dad's writing covers the pages. There are maps and drawings of salmon and trout, flies taped to the pages, pictures of water swelling around eddies.

"It's my fishing journal. I kept it for ten years on the secret spots and fish and the best flies for each. Since you were fishing the last time I was here, I thought it was time to give it to you."

"Thanks, Dad, but I really don't fish that much. Maybe I could share it with Dottie."

"I saved it for you," he says, touching the cover. I can tell he'd like to take it back. He's the angler. He's the one who could pull an eight-pound trout out of the middle of a rushing river muddied by glacier runoff.

"I'm just not a real fisherman."

"I wrote it for you. Just you," he says, and touches my cheek.

I open it to the front page, and there is a dedication to me, dated on my birthday.

*For Martha*, it reads. *Here is where I'll keep all my secrets. With all my love, Your Dad.*

"They're your secrets now," he says, and kisses me on my head.

"Thank you," I say, and wish he would stay just a second longer, but Gwen calls to him and he is gone, away from me. I have nothing for him. I didn't know he would be here, and mentally I go through my room, my closet, thinking of what I have that could compare and there is nothing. I have nothing for him. Mom smiles and moves close to me, turning the pages and touching each drawing with me.

The days get longer and the weather has decided on an easy winter. It snows at night, and the days hold sunny, clear skies. Because the glare from the snow is so bright, we Alaskans walk around with sunglasses on, and some get the suntans they long for the rest of the year. People come into the theater with red cheeks and pink noses and pale white eyes like raccoons.

"It's like Southern California in the winter," says Katherine. "Except in L.A., we'd be wearing shorts instead of seventeen layers."

"Sometimes, if the sun is really strong, and you're in a really bright patch of snow, it can be pretty warm. I've actually sweated. I'm sure some crazy person would wear shorts."

"Crazy for sure." Katherine has traded her high-heeled boots for a flat-bottomed pair with wool lining. She wears thermal undershirts, and occasionally she'll wear a flannel shirt. But she still wears her lipstick, and for this I am grateful.

And Mr. Martin wears full Hawaiian shirts in yellows so hot it hurts my eyes to watch him lecture. He wears blues the color of the sky, and oranges not found anywhere in nature. And for each day we get eight more minutes of sunshine. Those eight minutes soak into all of us, letting us face the next day with hope and faith that there will be more sun.

It is in this mood that letters start to come back to me. I've paid the extra money for advanced acceptance and included overnight envelopes. Some are sorry and perhaps I can resubmit to the regular application process. But some—Hawaii, San Diego, Florida—say yes.

I open each letter alone in my room. I open them slowly, touching each page, studying the pictures of sunshine and bathing suits and boats on crystal blue water.

I tell Mom when she gets home and Dottie and Gwen are studying.

"Mom, San Diego accepted me. And Hawaii and Florida."

"Good girl." She touches my cheek. "Thanks for picking the warm spots. I'm proud. So proud, but I don't want you to go."

"I don't want to either." And this is true because while I unwrap those catalogs and packets, I want to cry. No blue water or blond boys are even close to Alaska. The modern buildings and high-tech labs mean nothing to me.

"You have to, though. You're wasting away here."

"I know."

"It will be warm, wherever you go. You can get a suntan."

"Maybe."

# spring

As the days lengthen, Ben stays with Katherine a night or a whole weekend. I go to the theater after school and the sun is still up and bright in the sky and Katherine and Ben sit behind the register tying flies. Her hands are tangled in wire and pipe cleaner.

"I'll never get this right."

"You're doing great. Martha, tell her she's doing great."

"Looks awesome." But no salmon will hit that.

And then he leaves town for a while and Katherine is quiet, watching the bay and waiting for him to come back.

"It's the way with Alaska men," I tell her on a day when the bay is clear and all but the top of Iliamna is covered in clouds. The glacier across the bay blankets the side of a mountain and calves all year. Some months, if it is cold enough in the bay, those icebergs will float across and land on the spit.

"Crappy," she says. She puts her arm around me. "You're a great friend. And a great employee."

"Thank you," I say, not feeling that great because I haven't told her that I am really leaving and then she'll be here alone. And I'm not a great friend, because I like it when Ben leaves and it is just me and her and my secret is truly safe.

We prepare the theater. We're showing eighties movies this week, and it's brought out all the hippie kids who camp on the spit and shower and wash their clothes at the Laundromat. The girls file in and hand me sandy, crumpled dollar bills and tell me these movies are their favorites.

"I saw it in the theater. I didn't realize how old I was until today," says a girl with her long blond hair knotted into dreads.

"You're my Jake Ryan," she says to the guy next to her. He wears dreads too, but his are woven with hot pink and green yarn.

He shrugs. "Happily," he says.

"You don't even know who I'm talking about. *Sixteen Candles*. 'Make a wish, Samantha,'" she says. "You know, right?" she asks me.

"I do," I say, thinking of that night with Steven. I hand her the popcorn. She sprinkles the yeast Katherine has started carrying along with the salt and extra butter flavoring.

"Cool," he says, and kisses her smudged cheek.

Katherine disappears when the line lightens, and later I find her in the theater, in the back row, mouthing the words to the movie, and she gets it line for line. And I wonder if she is really happy here. What are the things she misses? When I am gone, maybe in San Diego, I'll have the things she misses, and she'll have the things I miss, but will either of us appreciate it?

Days grow warmer and we wear sweatshirts and jeans and a vest. The days are normal length. Two times a year it happens. It's natural, so no one really notices.

Mr. Hale calls and tells Mom that he will be at our house next week. He's bringing a man from Anchorage.

"We just need some answers," he says.

Mom calls Dad. "I'll be there," he says.

"Okay," she says. "Thank you."

Dad arrives the night before. He dresses different. He wears khakis and an ironed, buttoned shirt.

"Dad, you aren't meeting the president," Dottie teases. Gwen presses the creases in his pants between her small fingers, trying to make them even sharper.

"Marty," he says, and hugs me. "How are you doing?"

"Well," I say, "I'm going to college."

"Which one?"

"Not sure."

"Congratulations."

"Thank you, Dad." I hug him again and he is startled. I never do that.

When the house is quiet, I open my window and climb out. I set out across the field that separates my house from

Steven's. As I go, I smell the sharp green scent of new fire-weed shoots as they are crushed under my feet.

"I'm sorry, fireweed," I say, feeling like Gwen and wishing there were a better way, but I'm halfway there and so I continue, and when I get there, the lock is bright and shiny and new. And I go around the house, and the windows too have been replaced with double-paned glass. I cup my hand to my eyes and see inside in the bright blue moonlight. There is a pile of business cards on the counter, and the floors shine. This must have happened during my days at school, or my nights at the theater. Steven's house is no longer his, and it is no longer mine.

"Okay," I say, fogging the window. "I understand." And as I turn I see the three sisters, Iliamna, Redoubt and the faint glow that's Spurr, and each is lit by the same hot blue moon, pulsing again like they did so long ago, ready for spring, for life to start again.

Mr. Hale brings a man the next day. It is a Saturday, and so we are all off, but Dad has taken Gwen to a friend's. Mom makes coffee and sets out corn muffins. She wears an apron. And when he returns, Dad reads a newspaper. This is the way we want to be seen.

Mr. Hale introduces the man from Anchorage as Mr. Winter. Dottie smirks and I know there will be a joke after he leaves.

Mr. Winter explains that this is not an investigation of me. "We just want to know what's happening to our hunters. We want to keep people safe. We need to know what we're missing," he says, sipping his coffee.

He wears a pressed work shirt and new boots. His nails are clean and almost shine. He's lived in Anchorage too long, if his nails are that perfect.

"We weren't hunting."

"I know. You were camping, and fishing. But Steven Handell was a hunter. He had a license and had taken a number of state-sponsored classes."

Hearing this man say Steven's full name is jarring. He pauses before saying it, as if reading it off an index card, like the principal did at Steven's graduation.

"The other men who were shot also took classes; they all had licenses. As I looked over the file, I saw that Steven was an excellent marksman."

Mr. Hale nodded. "He and my son often went to the gun range for practice."

"Even the best shots miss," says Dottie. She is sitting close to me at the table, her leg warm against mine.

"I think all of us have had a close call. One time, I was about to take a shot, and a gnat buzzed into my ear. Gave me a heart attack. A gnat," Dad says, and I wonder how much Mom told him over coffee last night while I helped Gwen with her homework.

"He was an excellent shot," I say. Steven had patience behind the scope of a rifle. I too had seen him at the firing range, shots ringing all around him. And when his clay pigeon was released he breathed once, twice, and as the disk began to drop and I was sure he'd lost his shot, he pulled the trigger. Clay exploded and scattered into the sky.

"He'd just graduated, right?" asks Mr. Winter. I nod.

"Did he have any plans?"

"Many," I said.

"Did he seem upset out there to you? It is an upsetting time for any kid."

"No, he was fine. Chinitna Bay was his favorite."

"Why did you go?" Mr. Winter asks, and I have to pause. How can I say that he was showing me his heaven? His beauty? This Anchorage man could never know.

"A girl wants to be alone with her boyfriend for the weekend. Should she spell it out?" Dottie, again. I grab her knee under the table, expecting Mom to send her out. But Mom is quiet and looks at Mr. Winter as if Dottie has asked a legitimate question.

Mr. Winter clears his throat, also expecting someone to help him, but Dottie just stares. He takes another sip of coffee and clears his throat and he asks the real question.

"Where were you when it happened?"

"Close," I say, which in a way is the truth.

"How close? Twenty yards? Twenty feet?"

"I'm bad with that."

"From here to the door? As close as we are now?"

"Umm. I can't really remember." My first lie. How could I forget? In my memory not only do the moments after stretch on, but also the seconds before. Steven's arms around mine. His breath in my ear.

"Okay, count to three and exhale." His voice.

"How much did you see?" the man asks.

His hands over mine, the gun steady. An empty soda can on a rock far away. Steven's thumb, a small cut. I wonder where he got it.

"I was looking away," I say. "I was picking watermelon berries."

"Watermelon berries?" the man asks.

"Berries. They're red, shaped like a watermelon. They taste like watermelon. That's what we Alaskans call them," Dottie snaps.

"Dorothy," Dad says, and shakes his head. He closes his eyes.

They taste just like watermelons, and I never liked them, but they were Steven's favorite. I'd picked a creel-full before he decided I needed practice.

"What if a bear comes and I'm not around? What if you really do decide to be crazy and move here with me? We're total sustenance living here. You need to shoot," he said. And I'd been saying no all along because my family has never had a gun. Mom says we don't need one. We live in a big town. No bears, and we're smart girls. We don't wander right up to a moose as if it were a horse.

"I'm not going to shoot a gun," I said. "I'll just be careful."

"You can't be here with me without knowing how to shoot," he said. "It isn't safe."

"Later," I said, running my hands over his stomach.

"I saw a black bear on the beach this morning. I think now is a good time." His eyes darkened to a deeper blue, which meant he was serious. I couldn't change his mind.

"Okay, as long as you don't laugh."

"I won't." He bit at his bottom lip and kissed me on the nose. My last kiss. It was quick, and when his lips left my skin, there was a tiny wet spot right on the tip.

"Do you have any CPR training, Martha? Do you have any life-saving training? Did Steven?" the man asks.

"We had a first aid kit. We had a satellite phone."

"I see that you used both, but why did Steven think it was okay for you to be there when you had no training?"

"If he'd been alone in the bush, there would have been no one to help anyway," Mom says.

He might as well have been alone. If he had, he would have returned to me. He would have brought me salmon, fresh caught. He would have brought me a river rock, perfectly smooth and round, the color of his eyes.

"We think perhaps we need to add a lifesaving course to the hunting license requirements. It could help."

"The boy was shot in the gut. There's no amount of lifesaving that could have helped. She did what she could," Dad says. So Mom has told him everything, but he is still here and so I smile a little smile at him when he catches my eye.

"I recognize that the injury was fatal, but not all are like this," Mr. Winter says. "We had a death during moose season last year where a man was shot in the arm but died because the other hunter didn't know how to tie a tourniquet."

Steven positioned my arms, inhaled and exhaled. "Hold still," he said, and removed his arms from mine. He stepped to my left, and in that second, my arms dropped just enough under the weight of the heavy rifle. I squeezed the trigger and the gun jerked back and the can never moved, and then I heard a small ping like a quarter dropped into a vending machine. The bullet ricocheted from the rock that held the soda can and changed course. At first there was nothing. No blood, no sound. And then Steven: "I'm okay."

Seconds later, blood on his hands. Kneeling beside him, I found blood on my hands. I called for help on the satellite phone. Called the floatplane company because it was the only number I could find. They sent someone. They said it would be an hour at least.

"We'll be there," the man said, and there was a pause on the line. Static. "We'll be there."

They came days later, but really in about forty-five minutes. They'd already been in the air with a fishing party. They landed and left the party there, on our bay. The men lifted Steven's body into the plane. I touched the rock, a single metallic scrape. One woman in waders and fishing jacket held me. "I'll gather your things," she said. "I'll get them all." She kissed me on the forehead, and when I couldn't move, my feet planted on the rocks of the beach, she tried to take the gun, but I wouldn't let go. She grabbed my arm and pulled me to the plane. She pushed me through the door.

I never saw them again, but I found all of our things days later, bundled together in a corner of my garage.

"I know you did all you could. We just want to help other people," Mr. Winter says. "If you can think of anything, please let us know." He hands me a business card and stands.

It's over.

The men shake hands with Dad, and Mom shows them to the door. Dottie rubs my earlobe between her fingers. "You did great. So strong."

"Thanks. I'm tired now."

"I understand." She stands and offers me her hand and we walk to my bedroom, where she pulls the blankets up to my chin and kisses me on the head, like we do when Gwen is sick and too tired to sleep.

I close my eyes and Dad walks in after Dottie has left.

"Hey," he breathes. "You awake?"

"No," I say, and roll over.

"Then why are you talking, Miss Martha?"

"Sleeptalking, like sleepwalking."

"Listen, I'll come back as often as you want. Mom and I want you to be safe, and to feel safe."

"I'm good. Thank you for being here." I roll back to him and he's changed from his business clothes to his Alaska clothes. A hole is fraying at the elbow of his wool shirt.

"Those big-city guys. They see a houseful of women and think they can just bulldoze through. But really, I didn't do anything. Your mom and your sisters and you—you guys are the strong ones here. You are the ones keeping it all together."

"Barely."

"It always feels that way. When will you know about school?" He puts his hand in mine and I see another resemblance between us. Our hands are the same shape, fingers thin, nails pointy.

"You'll be the first person I tell."

"Good," he says, and kisses me on the cheek. "You rest now. I'm going home tomorrow."

"I'll say goodbye."

"Okay," he says, and leaves my room and I finally sleep.

When I wake in the middle of the night, to a purple sky and a yellow moon, I find my mother sleeping next to me. Her body is perfectly curled around mine, and I close my eyes and sleep again.

We eat the breakfast that Dottie and Gwen have made. Chocolate chip pancakes with lopsided happy faces in them.

"Gwen made family portraits in the pancake medium," Dottie says, handing the warmed syrup around.

"Our daughter has a gift," Dad says, and buries his face in Gwen's hair. She crosses her eyes and sticks out her tongue and then laughs a big, deep laugh for such a small girl.

"She's postmodern," Mom says.

We eat and Dad leaves after the dishes have been cleared and he's washed them wearing a frilly apron Dottie has dug out of somewhere.

He hugs each of us, and when he gets to me, I whisper the name of a place in his ear. He smiles and kisses me on the cheek.

"There's a direct flight from Anchorage," he whispers back.

I don't tell him that I already know, that I called the airlines to find out which college would be easiest for everyone to visit, and for me to fly home from just as quickly.

Now that winter has broken and spring is here, people begin tramping through Steven's house. I watch them as they pull up the drive and the Realtor waves. Some are couples with rental cars and they dress the part, but their jeans are just a bit too dark and their shirts too pressed. These couples smile and wave back, and when they walk out, they are not quite as chipper. I think they have a place in mind that comes predecorated with plaid couches and a fire lit, and maybe they hope the previous tenants forgot a mounted fish or caribou on the wall.

And men come too. They pull up in big, rusted trucks with gun racks inside. They are looking for a fishing cabin near the Anchor River. A cabin the wife can roost in and feel at home. And when the men leave, they nod and shake the Realtor's hand and drive away, kicking up gravel and fishtailing down the road.

A single woman looks, and I know she will be the one to take it. She drives a station wagon, rusted at the wheel wells, and she has an Alaska plate. She gets out and calls hello to the Realtor over the roof of the car. She pauses and leans in the back and unbuckles a baby from the car seat. The woman wears overalls and tennis shoes and as she walks to the house, she stops and stares at the view. She faces the baby around and bounces it, whispers in its ear and turns to the house, then opens the door without waiting for the Realtor.

They are in there for a long time, and when she leaves, she faces the bay once more. And later in the night, she returns without the Realtor, the baby snuggled into a sling across her chest, and she sits on the deck where Steven and I stood so many times to recite the mountains, Steven pointing to bays and inlets and glaciers. This woman sits, unmoving, and when the sun goes down, she leaves and I breathe a sigh of relief. At least the view will still be watched.

And now the days are warm. Dottie is often gone with Sean. Gwen has various practices and extra classes at school, and Mom is working more. The town is excited. People wave on the street and smile, and the brave Alaskans wear shorts during the day.

And everyone comes to the movies. We're showing two a day now. One in the afternoon and a different one at night, and everyone comes to both. We show a cartoon for the kids, and each time I come to work for the afternoon show, Katherine shakes her head and whispers to me, "I don't know how these parents do it, sitting there through a whole two-hour cartoon."

"It's not two hours."

"Whatever, it feels like ten." She smiles and points as another little kid runs into the lobby looking for the bathroom. "Little demons," she says.

And Mr. Martin is toning down his shirts. He's back in long sleeves, and as I sit in his class, the trees out the window are more green than brown. They are still infected, but more are stronger, and younger, ready to battle the beetles.

After class, Mr. Martin pauses in front of my desk.

"I saw your name on the list in the counselor's office. It's a great school. Perfect for you," he says, tapping an eraser on my table. I nod.

"You're making me proud, and Steven too."

"Thanks, Mr. Martin."

"No problem. Just remember us in the wintertime."

"You'll have to come and visit, pick up some more shirts."

"Will do. Now go and finish your homework."

"Thanks," I say, and grab my bag. I put one arm around him and squeeze. I'll miss him more than any of them. He laughs and blushes and I run out the door. Off to work. As

I drive from school to the theater, my stomach knots. I don't want to tell her everything. I don't want to tell her that I'm leaving her too.

I find her sitting on the bench someone years ago made from a felled tree. The bench looks out over Pioneer Street and over the bay to the glaciers.

"What's up?" I say, and sit next to her.

"Getting some sun. I think my vitamin D level is low."

"It's dangerous, sitting in the sun too long. You'll get all hyper if you get too much vitamin D."

"I'm feeling pretty calm right now." She turns to me and smiles. Her skin is translucent, her lips naturally pink. Alaska is doing her good.

"Theater's okay?"

"Actually yes, we're doing better than before I bought it," she says, and looks back out over the water.

"Must be the popcorn," I say.

A breeze comes off the water, and it's fresh like a good rain. The greatest air purifier in the world, Dad always says. I grow warm sitting beneath the high sun.

"I think we're just showing more movies." She stretches out her arms and legs. She's wearing her tall boots again. And in the light, her hair glistens black and her gray streak shines white.

I take a breath. "Katherine, I need to tell you something."

"I hate it when people who need to tell me something preface it with that."

"Okay. I'll just say it. I'm going to school."

"You should have already been."

"No, I'm going to college."

She rubs her eyes and turns again to me and smiles. "Congratulations. Where to?"

"Hawaii accepted me into the marine biology program. I figure it's a lot like here, but just warm."

"And an island."

"Living in Homer is sort of like living on an island. It takes forever to get anywhere, so it kind of isn't worth leaving."

She nods and puts her hand on mine. "It's lovely there. Lush, of course, and tropical. You're right, it's a lot like here. Congratulations for real."

"I looked at the pictures, and if it weren't for the people in swimsuits roasting pigs, the green looked like Alaska." Rolling hills of brush, wildflowers in the summer. Volcanoes.

"You'll have no shortage of visitors."

"There's a direct flight from Anchorage to Honolulu."

"I'll be sure to book my ticket. Soon I'll have my first Permanent Fund check."

"Lots of travel specials then."

"Will you learn to surf?"

"Maybe."

"Well, Gidget, don't break too many hearts. Maybe you'll find a Moon Doggie."

"Real Alaska girls have no time for surfer boys."

She smiles, but her eyebrows crease and tears fill her eyes. "I'll miss you. Why does everyone leave the cold?"

I hug her. "I have to leave."

"No you don't. You want to. And who can blame you?"

"No, Katherine." I pull back. "I really do need to leave. There was a boy here. And he's gone now because of me.

But he's still here in so many ways that I can't be here anymore."

She shakes her head at me. I've been unclear. I have to try again.

"He's dead, Katherine. He was my boyfriend. And he's dead now. He died across the bay. An accident. When I was there." I stop and she breathes deeply. I match my breath to hers. "People wonder why I didn't save him."

I look out at the bay. It's calm and blue. You'd never know that right about now, a current moves beneath the surface, pulling and pushing tons of water to the ocean. "And it's my fault."

"I can't believe that." She purses her lips and wipes her face, then looks back across the bay.

"Believe me. You really have no choice."

"I do," she says, and looks at me again. "I'm sorry. And if leaving will stop you from blaming yourself, then you do need to go."

I stand and pull her up. I've never noticed until this moment that even in her tall boots, Katherine is shorter than I am. I hook my arm through hers.

"The show must go on," I say as we head back to the theater.

"It's a new movie. Pirates, swashbuckling."

"Be my date?"

"I'd be honored."

The crowd is large. Katherine hands out eye patches to the kids in line, and some of the adults too. She puts one over her own eye. The woman who owns the fancy breakfast place comes in, and they joke about the other night when they went to a bar on the spit. And Ben surprises her.

She smiles and touches her lips, remembering her lipstick. He offers money as he walks in, but she waves it away. He says something that I can't hear over the popcorn machine. She laughs. He kisses her cheek as he walks past her and into my line.

"Hey," he says, and leans over the counter to kiss my cheek.

"I'm going to school, Ben."

"Oh yeah? Anyplace I want to visit?"

"Hawaii."

"Perfect," he says, taking popcorn. "I'll save a seat for the both of you."

When the line has died, Katherine serves popcorn for us both and reaches under the counter for the grenadine.

"The hard stuff," she says, and pours us each a Shirley Temple. "To a couple of girls." She holds up her paper cup.

"To us. The finest movie babes in town."

We press our cups together, then pull back the heavy curtain and take seats in the back row next to Ben.

# summer

Fishing season is open, silvers first, then pinks. King salmon for just a few days. Dottie and I go a few times and I let her lead the way. She ties my flies and shows how and where to cast. I don't bring Dad's notebook, because she knows the lessons in there by heart. They are in her blood. She doesn't need a book.

We ride mountain bikes in and fish the Russian River. The bushes are dense and there are signs warning of bears. I watch her as she fishes, her legs spread apart, her cast long, the line flowing in a perfect arc behind her and snapping out and landing in a calm area in the center of the rushing river.

"Fish on!" she calls again and again, reeling them in without snapping a single one off. She keeps none of them.

"Go on and make more fishies for me to catch," she says as she lets them go.

I catch some too, when I've cast just as perfectly as she has. Some bite line and pop off. And sometimes, when Dottie is far enough downriver so she can't see, I just let my line drift and I stand in the cold water, feeling the smooth river rock under my waders, and I just stare at the green, at the hot purple fireweed and the pale purple monkshood, and at the fish, silver flashes under the clear water.

"Strip," Dottie calls when she catches me staring. My fly has caught on a rock, not fooling a single fish. "They're going to get wise to us," she says, pulling my line in and biting off the hook and fly. "We need to change you up. I think because of the clouds and the current—"

"We need a deeper orange egg pattern," I say, completing her sentence.

She pauses. "Wow, you're right."

"Hey, I'm an Alaskan too." Though I would have never known about the pattern if I hadn't been up last night cribbing from Dad's book.

And just days before I leave, I take Katherine out again. We go back to Cooper Landing. It is so early in the season there are no dead fish lying on the banks, and as we cross the river in the ferry I look upstream and the water is still a deep, cloudy blue. I'm grateful for the glaciers and the runoff and that I'll always be reminded of the color of his eyes.

Katherine's waders look well used, and she ties on

without help. Both of us cast out and catch rockfish. We talk and laugh and both of us hook up. We each reel in a beautiful silver, the color bright, shiny.

"I have my camera," she says, and we take pictures.

"With the photos, we can have them mounted."

"Awesome," she says. And I take my knife and brain them both. Katherine guts them with no instruction from me and we put them in our cooler.

"Look at us," she says, and does a little dance. Fish scales make her hands glint in the sunlight.

"We're so tough," I say.

And we catch some more rock and stick fish and even a can fish and call it a day. On the drive back, I play a CD Steven made me.

"Play it while I'm gone," he'd said before he left for a weekend in a moose blind.

There are songs by a man who played a guitar and sang the saddest songs I've ever heard. He killed himself a few years after he recorded them. And Katherine knows the words.

"How do you know this?" I ask.

"Old favorite."

"Sad, huh?"

"Sad." She pauses and looks out the window. The green trees, fireweed and blue sky open wide, waiting. "Someone always has to leave."

I nod, whispering the song's lyrics with her.


My last night in Alaska and I've said my goodbyes—to my teachers and to the kids in my classes. I said goodbye to the whale. I stood beneath its skeleton, warm and gold in the afternoon light.

"Thank you," I said, because the whale has given me so much. It gave me Steven and a way out of Alaska when I needed one. But if it hadn't been for that whale, I wouldn't have to leave. I could stay in Alaska, fishing and working at the theater, and maybe when the time was better, I would find a different whale with better luck attached.

"Bye, whale." The salty, sea smell of its bones filled my nose again and my fingers itched from the coarse sandpaper of its joints.

And on my last night, I say goodbye to Steven. The woman has bought the house and she's begun moving in. She brings boxes during the day, but leaves in the evening. Late, late, when there is finally darkness, I go to his house, screwdriver in hand. I pop his window off and climb into his bedroom. There are boxes piled in one corner, and in the moonlight I can see that she's painted the walls silvery purple, and she's drawn bees and flowers and butterflies on the walls. On the ceiling, whole constellations glow.

It's not my room anymore. And Steven is gone. No need for a goodbye, and so I crawl back out and press the window back in. And as I turn I see my mountains, the three sisters. But I can't say goodbye to them, and so I walk through the fireweed and into my house, where my bags are packed and my room is perfectly clean. Already waiting for me to come back.

# Hawaii

**The four of us go to Hawaii—they'll drop me off at** school. Dottie brings the smallest suitcase—"What more do I need besides some shorts and bikinis?" And I suppose she's right.

"Is it true there are bugs the size of my thumb?" Gwen asks on the airplane.

"You have very small thumbs," I say. "At home we have banana slugs. They're the size of your finger."

"But these bugs fly," she says.

We settle in and Mom sits next to me. She keeps her hand on me the whole flight. And once during the movie, she leans over to me and whispers, "I'm not ready for you to go."

I can't respond, because if I do I will make them turn the plane around and head back home.

It's evening when we land, and the heat hits us like a brick wall. I've never known humidity like this, the kind where you feel like you can't take a breath. But the air smells sweet like blooming flowers.

And in the hotel, we sleep with the windows open and that same sweet, warm air blows over me all night. We wake and slather on sunscreen. Dot and Gwen get ready for a day in the sun and the sand.

"We're bathing beauties today," Dottie says.

"I'm going to bury myself in the sand," Gwen says.

"Just remember to put sunblock on," Mom says. "Dot, please put it on your sister once an hour."

"Mother," Dottie says.

"Blame yourself, Dottie," Mom says. "Your hair spray last year alone totally obliterated the ozone layer."

Dottie rolls her eyes again and grabs Gwen and their beach bags, and they leave.


Mom and I wander the campus, finding my classes, books, various offices. And there are others like me, pale kids with pink cheeks sweating in the sun. I smile at a couple of people my age, and Mom chats with other mothers as we wander.

We find my room. A suite, they call it, but this is no hotel. A bunk bed, two desks and a bathroom we'll share with the other two girls in the room next to ours.

"It's kind of like home. You slept in the same room with Dottie when Gwen came along, until we turned the study into your room," Mom says.

I look out the window and onto campus. People milling everywhere.

"If you lean over and look left, you can see a bit of the ocean," someone says behind me. I pull back and turn to find a girl my height, standing with her hands on her hips. She's tanned the color of a nut, with short black hair.

"I'm your roommate," she says, "Kiana." She holds out her hand and I take it.

"Good to meet you."

"Seriously, check out the view. You can't beat it in this dorm."

We lean out together and there it is, the ocean. Just a sliver, but enough to see the white waves breaking onto the beach, sand as white as milk.

"Very cool."

"We lucked out," Kiana says, and introduces herself to my mom. "Don't worry, your girl will be well taken care of. My mom is already planning to have her to dinner this week."

"Your family lives here, but you live in the dorms?" Mom asks, laughing.

"I do. *Kama'aina*. It means from the land. Real Hawaiians."

"We're from Alaska," I say, and Kiana laughs.

Mom and I unpack, and Kiana lies on her bed.

"Yes," she says, "there really are flying bugs the size of your thumb."

"No," I say, "it isn't twenty-four hours of night where I live."

Soon I'm all unpacked and I spend one last night with my family. And the next day all of them come with me to school to drop me off for good. They're back in jeans and they carry warm jackets. Mom and my sisters walk me to my room; Kiana has gone to her first class. I hug Gwen. "See you later," she says, and gives me wet kisses on my cheeks and forehead and eyelids.

Dottie holds me tight. I breathe her in, coconut from her tanning lotion, a rose smell from her makeup, and the green smell of her hair, Alaska never really washed from it.

And Mom, who smiles and grabs my shoulders. "You'll be great. I'm so excited for you." And I cry again. But it's not like those days after Steven. I know I'll stop soon. Mom hugs me and kisses my head and she herds my sisters out of my room and down the hall and back to Alaska. And then I am alone. For once. I lean out the window and watch the ocean, breathing in the air, clean like a rain. Very close to home.

# epilogue

And so this is what happened. I did study marine biology.
Kiana's family became an extension of my own. She came
with me to Alaska a few times. And there were boys. Cute
boys, Hawaiian boys, a boy from Minnesota who could understand about missing snow. But I fell in love with none of
them. And that's okay.

Dottie is gone from Alaska too. She broke up with Sean,
and she lives in Los Angeles. She goes to school and she
bartends and she does makeup for weddings and commercials. She comes to visit every few months.

Katherine still owns the theater, and Ben lives with her.
She still wears tall boots, and her lipstick sometimes, but

her jeans are worn and she now has fish mounted on the walls of the theater. Her fish.

Kiana and I live in a shack in Hana, Maui, which is a two-hour drive on a one-lane road from Kapalua. I work for a small group studying the whales as they migrate from Hawaii to Alaska. We slosh around in boats and take notes about size and sex. And we write reports to our colleagues in Alaska. We tell them which whales to expect, and they report on the ones that showed up. It's good work. When the whales get close to our boats, I lean over, my hand in the water, and tell them to say hello to Alaska for me.

"Tell the fireweed I miss it. Tell Iliamna and Redoubt and Spurr hello. Tell the whales to come back," I say. "Give Mom and Gwen a kiss."

Kiana is studying to becoming a chef at a hotel. And when we aren't working, we surf. Surfing in Hana is like fishing in Alaska. There is quiet and the water and the green, and there is me in the middle of it all.

The water passes beneath me, lifting me up and over, giving me a better view of the waterfalls deep in the cliffs.

Another wave comes, and I paddle, but not too hard because I am quiet and waiting and watching the beauty.